MARIE-HÉLÈNE LEBEAULT
AUTHOR OF THE EVERS SERIES

A CURSE OF
THORNS
AND
SLUMBER

A SLEEPING BEAUTY RETELLING

BEACHES AND TRAILS
PUBLISHING

CHAPTER 1

A THIEF'S CHOICE

The moon was high, casting long, silvery shadows over the narrow streets of Solstraea's capital. Liora moved like a wraith between buildings, the weight of the stolen jewels tugging at the pouch strapped to her side. Her heart pounded in rhythm with her swift steps, each footfall light and deliberate. She knew the patrols' schedules down to the second—it wasn't her first time in the Upper Market. But it might be her last.

Rounding a corner, she came face-to-face with a guard, his torchlight flickering over her face. His eyes widened, and before he could call out, Liora dove into the nearest alley, her breath sharp in her throat. Her fingers itched for the dagger at her belt, but she pushed the thought away. Running had always worked better than fighting. She darted between crates and barrels, the jewels clinking faintly with each step.

But then she heard it—the unmistakable sound of metal boots, more than one pair, approaching fast. *Trapped.* Panic clawed at her chest. The alleyway she had chosen was a dead end. Cursing under her breath, she spun, searching for a way out. A gate, a window, anything.

Nothing.

The guards closed in, their torches casting long shadows along the stone walls, flickering like the dreams she once had of escape. Liora pressed herself against the wall, trying to melt into the darkness. Her breathing slowed, her heart pounding in her ears. She could still fight, but against how many? Two? Three? She'd be lucky if they took her in alive.

"Stop right there!" A rough voice echoed through the alley, followed by the heavy clank of armor.

Liora's jaw clenched. *Caught.*

Before she could make her decision, a hand closed around her arm with iron force, dragging her into the open. She kicked back instinctively, aiming for the gap in the guard's armor at his knee, but his grip didn't falter. The others joined him, surrounding her in a circle of flickering light.

"Liora Thornhand," one of the guards sneered, his voice dripping with disdain. "Back to your old tricks, I see."

She spat on the ground near his feet, lifting her chin defiantly. "If you were better at your job, maybe I wouldn't get so many chances."

His face darkened, but before he could retaliate, another voice broke through. "Enough."

A woman stepped forward from the shadows, her figure draped in a long, dark cloak. Her eyes gleamed under the hood, sharp as the blade Liora still clutched at her side. Liora didn't recognize her—not a guard, not a noble.

The woman's gaze lingered on Liora, calculating. "You're coming with me."

Liora's stomach dropped. "I don't think so."

"You don't have a choice," the woman said coolly, stepping closer. "But you'll want to hear what I have to say."

Liora hesitated. Something in the woman's voice sent a chill up her spine. She was dangerous, but not in the same way as the guards. There was power in her—power that Liora didn't want to test.

The guards shifted, waiting for an order. When the woman nodded, they seized Liora's arms. She struggled, but it was pointless; they were too strong, and there were too many. The woman gestured, and they pulled Liora along, dragging her toward the palace at the city's heart.

———

They led her through the towering gates of the palace and into a wide, dimly lit chamber that smelled faintly of smoke and ancient tomes. She knew this was no ordinary holding cell. The moment the guards stepped back, releasing her arms, Liora turned to face the woman who had brought her here.

"What do you want?" Liora demanded, trying to keep the fear out of her voice. "If this is about the jewels, I—"

"It's not about the jewels," the woman interrupted, her tone sharp but calm. She pulled back her hood, revealing dark, silver-threaded hair and eyes that seemed to pierce straight through Liora's defenses. "My name is Callia. I'm a mage of the court."

Liora's heart sank further. *A mage.* She knew better than to underestimate them. Mages were feared for good reason, even by thieves like her.

Callia stepped forward, studying Liora with a cold intensity. "You have a gift, Liora. A rare one."

Liora's instinct was to deny it, but she kept silent. The mages always knew too much.

"We've been watching you," Callia continued. "Your ability to control thorns is not something to be squandered. It could save the kingdom."

Liora narrowed her eyes, heart pounding. "Save the kingdom? I'm a thief, not a heroine."

Callia smiled faintly, but it didn't reach her eyes. "You don't need to be a heroine. You just need to follow orders. Prince Kael is dying. His heart is locked inside a magical rose, and only someone with your ability—someone marked by thorns—can reach it."

Liora stared at her. *The prince?* She hadn't seen him since before the curse, but rumors of his eternal sleep had spread far beyond the palace walls. His curse had left the kingdom leaderless, and the shadow of uncertainty had loomed over Solstraea for years.

"And what happens if I refuse?" Liora asked, her voice steady despite the storm building inside her.

Callia's smile vanished. "Refuse, and you'll be tried for your crimes. No more deals. No more escapes."

The weight of the decision settled on Liora like a suffocating cloak. The jewels she'd stolen seemed insignificant now compared to the gravity of the offer being placed before her. Breaking a curse? Entering some dream world to find a prince's heart?

She hated the feeling of being trapped, but more than that, she hated the idea of failing.

"What's the catch?" Liora asked, folding her arms.

"You might not survive," Callia replied simply. "The Dreamplane is dangerous, and the magic within it is unpredictable. But you'll have a chance. A better one than most."

Liora let out a slow breath, weighing her options. *Rot in a cell or face a nightmare.*

"Fine," she said, meeting Callia's gaze. "I'll do it."

Callia nodded, satisfaction flickering in her expression. "Good. Then prepare yourself, Liora. You'll enter the Dreamplane at dawn."

The dim light of early morning filtered through the high windows of the chamber. Liora stood before the circle of mages, her heart thudding against her ribs. Callia was at the center, surrounded by arcane symbols etched into the stone floor, glowing faintly with a soft, silver light. Liora shifted uncomfortably. The air felt heavy with magic, and every instinct she had told her to run.

But there was no turning back.

"Step into the circle," Callia instructed, her voice steady, almost casual, as if sending someone into a cursed prince's dream was a routine affair.

Liora took a deep breath and obeyed, her boots making a soft click against the cold stone. The moment she entered the circle, she felt it—an invisible force pressing against her skin, like stepping into the eye of a storm. The world outside the circle felt distant, muffled, as if she were sinking underwater.

"You'll be entering the Dreamplane, a world shaped by the prince's mind," Callia explained, her hands beginning to weave intricate patterns in the air. Silver threads of magic followed her movements, swirling around the circle. "Once inside, your task is to find the rose that holds his heart. Only you can release it, but beware—time moves differently there, and the longer you stay, the more dangerous it becomes."

Liora clenched her fists at her sides, her palms already damp with sweat. "And how do I get out?"

Callia paused, her eyes locking with Liora's. "When the heart is free, the prince will wake. If you fail... you won't."

Helpful, Liora thought bitterly, but kept her mouth shut.

The magic in the air thickened, and the symbols on the floor flared bright. The circle of mages began to chant in low, rhythmic tones. Liora's vision blurred, and the world around her seemed to ripple. The floor beneath her feet fell away, replaced by nothing but a vast, endless blackness.

She was falling.

Her stomach lurched, and she reached out instinctively for something to grab, but there was nothing—just the sensation of being pulled downward, faster and faster, into the void.

Then, with a sudden jolt, she landed.

Liora blinked, disoriented. Her knees hit something solid and cold, and she steadied herself, hands pressing into rough, damp earth. The scent of roses hit her immediately, a sharp, sweet fragrance that clung to the air like a thick fog.

She pushed herself to her feet, eyes scanning her surroundings.

She was standing in the middle of a garden—but not one she recognized. The roses that surrounded her were unlike any she had ever seen, their petals an eerie, glowing white, their stems winding with dark, thorn-covered vines. They twisted and spiraled up tall iron trellises that formed strange, jagged shapes against the sky.

Above her, the sky itself looked wrong—too dark, too vast, as if it stretched into eternity without a single star.

The Dreamplane.

Liora swallowed hard, her heart still racing from the fall. Everything here felt too still, too quiet. Like the world was holding its breath.

She took a cautious step forward, her boots sinking slightly into the damp earth. The garden stretched out in all directions, a maze of twisting paths and towering, thorny walls.

"Alright," she muttered under her breath. "Now where's this cursed prince?"

Liora wound her way through the maze, her eyes darting warily over the roses as she passed. The thorns seemed to move, ever so slightly, as if they were alive, reaching toward her. She kept her distance, but the path ahead offered no clear direction, and she had no idea how long she had been walking.

Time, like everything else here, felt strange.

After what felt like hours, the thorny walls finally opened up into a wide clearing. At the center stood a towering rose bush, larger than any Liora had seen. Its twisted branches arched high into the sky, and nestled deep within the tangle of vines was a single glowing rose.

Her heart skipped a beat. *That must be it.*

But before she could take a step forward, something stirred at the base of the rose bush.

A figure, half-hidden in the shadows, stood slowly. He was tall, with dark hair falling just below his chin, dressed in clothes that looked like they belonged to another time— worn, faded, but finely made. His eyes, however, were the most striking—icy blue, with a depth that made Liora's breath catch for a moment.

She recognized him immediately. *Prince Kael.*

But there was something wrong. He looked... distant. His eyes were sharp, but they seemed to look through her, not at her.

"You," he said, his voice low and cold. "Who are you?"

Liora froze. She had been prepared for hostility, but something about the way he looked at her unsettled her. She straightened, forcing a smirk. "A thief, apparently. The mages sent me to break your curse."

Kael's expression hardened. He stepped forward, his gaze narrowing. "Another one," he muttered, half to himself. "How many more are they going to send before they realize it's useless?"

Liora crossed her arms. "So, I'm not the first. Good to know."

Kael didn't answer. He looked her over, his eyes flicking to the pouch at her side where she still kept the stolen jewels—though they felt utterly useless here. "Why should I believe you?"

"I don't care if you do," Liora shot back, her patience already thinning. "I'm not here for you, anyway. I'm here for the rose."

At this, Kael's eyes darkened, a flicker of something unreadable passing over his face. "The rose," he repeated, his voice softer now, almost bitter. "Of course."

Liora took a step toward the rose bush, but Kael moved suddenly, blocking her path. His eyes were sharper now, more focused. "You think it's that simple?" he asked, his voice low. "That you can just come here and take it?"

She frowned, her pulse quickening. "Isn't that the idea?"

Kael's lips curled into a humorless smile. "It's never that simple."

Before Liora could respond, the ground beneath them shifted. The earth trembled, and from the shadows at the edges of the clearing, something moved.

Her heart lurched as she saw them—dark, twisted shapes, emerging from the thorn walls, their forms flickering and shifting like smoke. They moved with unnatural grace, their eyes glowing a faint, malevolent red.

Liora's hands went instinctively to her belt, but there were no daggers, no weapons. *Of course not.* This was the Dreamplane. Nothing was as it should be.

Kael glanced over his shoulder, his expression unreadable. "They'll tear you apart."

Liora's fingers twitched. She could feel the pull of the thorns around her, their magic calling to her like an old friend.

She stretched out her hand, and the nearest thorny vine obeyed.

With a sharp snap, the vine broke free of the rose bush, curling through the air toward the nearest shadow creature. The creature let out a shriek, its form unraveling as the thorns wrapped around it, slicing through the darkness like a knife through fabric.

Kael's eyes widened, surprise flickering over his face. "You—"

Liora didn't wait for him to finish. She thrust her hand forward again, sending another vine after the second creature. This one collapsed in a swirling mass of black smoke as the thorns pierced its chest.

The remaining creatures hesitated, their glowing eyes flicking between Liora and Kael. For a moment, the clearing was silent, the tension hanging thick in the air.

Then, with a final screech, they dissolved into the shadows, vanishing as quickly as they had come.

Liora exhaled, her heart pounding in her chest. She turned to Kael, her eyes narrowed. "Still think I'm useless?"

Kael stared at her for a long moment, his expression unreadable. The hostility in his eyes had faded, replaced by something else—caution, maybe. Or curiosity.

"You're not like the others," he said finally, his voice quieter now.

Liora shrugged, trying to ignore the way her heart was still racing. "Guess not."

Kael's gaze shifted to the thorns that still hung in the air around them, their sharp points gleaming faintly in the dream-light. He frowned, his brow furrowing. "What are you?"

"Thief," Liora replied with a smirk, though it felt more like a shield than anything else. "But I already told you that."

Kael didn't smile. He studied her for another moment, then glanced at the towering rose bush behind him. "The rose isn't what you think," he said quietly. "And if you're here to break the curse, then we're going to have to work together."

Liora raised an eyebrow. "What, no more threats? No more trying to scare me off?"

Kael's lips twitched, but it wasn't quite a smile. "You're still here, aren't you?"

There was a pause, the silence between them heavy with unspoken tension.

Finally, Liora sighed, glancing at the twisted vines that surrounded them. "Fine. We work together. But if you try anything—"

Kael raised a hand in surrender. "I won't."

For the first time since she had arrived, Liora felt a strange, uneasy truce settle between them. It was fragile, and she didn't trust it. But for now, it would have to do.

CHAPTER 2
SECRETS OF THE
DREAMPLANE

The air in the Dreamplane was heavier now. As Liora and Kael moved through the twisting pathways of the rose garden, the ground beneath their feet seemed less solid, as if the world itself was fraying at the edges. It gave Liora a strange, uneasy feeling, as though she might slip through the earth at any moment.

Kael walked ahead, silent and distant, his eyes flicking over the landscape with an intensity that made her wonder what he was seeing—if he was seeing the same things she was. She couldn't quite shake the feeling that everything around them was somehow tied to him, a reflection of his mind, his memories.

Liora's footsteps slowed as they came to a narrow bridge of stone, arching over what appeared to be a bottomless abyss. Below them, the darkness churned, restless and alive.

Kael hesitated at the edge, his eyes narrowing as he stared down into the void.

"What's down there?" Liora asked, her voice hushed.

She couldn't explain why, but the sight of the churning darkness made her stomach twist.

Kael didn't answer for a long moment. Then, without looking at her, he muttered, "Nothing. But it shouldn't be there."

Liora frowned, her unease growing. "What do you mean?"

Kael's expression tightened. "The Dreamplane isn't a fixed place. It's... alive in a way. Shaped by memories, thoughts, and dreams. Right now, it's unraveling, losing coherence, because the magic sustaining it is failing."

Liora's stomach clenched as she glanced down into the dark churning abyss below them. "So it's part of the curse, too? Like it's tied to you?"

Kael nodded slowly, his voice thick with tension. "Exactly. The Dreamplane mirrors my state. As I grow weaker, the Dreamplane breaks down, piece by piece, memory by memory. If it collapses completely, everything tied to it—my past, the curse, and anyone inside— disappears."

He glanced over his shoulder at her, his eyes shadowed with something that looked like fear. "And once they're gone, so am I."

Liora's heart skipped a beat. She hadn't realized how close the curse had come to claiming him. She could see it now—the weariness in his eyes, the way his shoulders sagged slightly, as if he was carrying a burden too heavy for anyone to bear.

She opened her mouth to say something—anything— but the words caught in her throat.

Kael turned away, stepping onto the bridge. "Let's keep moving."

Liora followed, her footsteps echoing hollowly across the stone. But as they crossed, she couldn't help glancing down into the darkness again, wondering what memories Kael had already lost—and what it would cost them both to save him.

The bridge led them into another twisted garden, but this one felt more hostile than the last. The thorn-covered vines were thicker here, their sharp, dark spines curling in unnatural patterns, as if they were waiting to strike.

Liora clenched her fists, feeling the familiar tug of the thorns' magic under her skin. She had grown up among thorns—learned to control them, bend them to her will— but this place was different. These thorns felt... alive.

Kael slowed his pace, his eyes scanning the thorny walls with suspicion. "There's something wrong here."

"You think?" Liora muttered under her breath, keeping a wary eye on the vines that seemed to pulse with a faint, dark energy.

As they moved deeper into the garden, the path narrowed, forcing them closer to the thorny walls. Liora could feel the thorns brushing against her arms, tugging at the sleeves of her jacket like fingers trying to pull her in. She gritted her teeth and pushed them back with a flick of her wrist, the vines obeying her magic without resistance.

"Stay close," Kael said, his voice low. "These thorns...

they're not just part of the Dreamplane. They're connected to the curse."

Liora shot him a sideways glance. "And how do you know that?"

Kael's jaw tightened, but he didn't answer right away. Instead, he stepped closer to one of the vines, reaching out with a hesitant hand. As his fingers brushed the dark spines, the thorn trembled and pulled away, retreating into the wall with a faint hiss.

"They react to me," he said quietly, almost to himself. "It's as if they know who I am. As if they're waiting for something."

Liora frowned. "Waiting for what?"

Kael's eyes flicked to hers, but he didn't answer.

For a moment, the only sound was the soft rustling of the vines as they moved through the garden. Then, without warning, the thorns lashed out.

Liora barely had time to react before a vine wrapped around her ankle, yanking her off her feet. She hit the ground hard, her breath knocked out of her chest. Kael shouted something, but she couldn't hear him over the roar of her own pulse. The thorns were tightening around her legs, pulling her deeper into the twisted, writhing mass.

Panic surged through her, and she instinctively reached out with her magic. The thorns resisted, fighting back against her control. **They were alive.** And they wanted her.

"Liora!"

Kael's voice cut through the haze of panic, and she saw

him struggling against his own tangle of vines, his face pale with fear.

Her heart pounded in her chest as she focused her magic, pushing harder, forcing the thorns to bend to her will. Slowly, painfully, the vines began to loosen their grip, retreating back into the walls.

Liora gasped for air as she stumbled to her feet, her legs trembling beneath her. Kael was beside her in an instant, his hand gripping her arm to steady her.

"Are you alright?" he asked, his voice tight with concern.

She nodded, still catching her breath. "Yeah. Just… give me a second."

Kael's eyes were sharp, his grip firm but not painful. "We need to move. This place isn't safe."

Liora glanced at the retreating thorns, her pulse still racing. "Yeah. No kidding."

———

By the time they found a place to stop for the night, Liora's legs were aching, and her head was throbbing with the strain of keeping the thorns at bay. They had made it out of the cursed garden, but the feeling of being hunted still lingered, thick and oppressive in the air.

Kael led her to a small, crumbling tower tucked into the side of a cliff. It was barely standing, its stone walls cracked and weathered, but it was better than nothing. The inside was empty, save for a few scattered pieces of broken furniture and a narrow window that overlooked the dreamscape below.

Liora sat down on a dusty, half-broken bench, her body sagging with exhaustion. She watched as Kael moved to the window, his gaze distant and troubled.

For a moment, neither of them spoke.

Then Kael broke the silence. "The curse is spreading faster than I thought."

Liora blinked, sitting up straighter. "What do you mean?"

Kael didn't turn to face her. "The thorns. They weren't here before. Not like that. They're a sign of the curse getting stronger."

Liora frowned, her heart sinking. "How much time do we have?"

Kael's shoulders tensed. "Not long."

A heavy silence settled between them. Liora leaned back against the wall, her mind racing. The weight of the curse felt heavier now, more real. She hadn't realized how close they were to losing everything—not just Kael, but the kingdom, too.

"You're quiet," Kael said suddenly, his voice soft. "That's unusual."

Liora shot him a sidelong glance, though there wasn't much bite to it. "Just thinking."

"About what?"

"About how we're probably going to die," she said, half-joking, though the fear in her chest made it hard to laugh.

Kael's lips twitched, but it wasn't quite a smile. "Comforting."

They sat in silence for a while longer, the tension between them thick but not hostile. It was strange, Liora thought, how quickly the dynamic between them had shifted. They were still strangers in a way, but there was a growing sense of... something. Not quite trust, but something close.

Kael glanced at her, his gaze unreadable in the fading light. "Why did you agree to this? To come here?"

Liora hesitated. "Does it matter?"

"It does to me."

She met his gaze, her throat tightening. She had told herself that she didn't care about him—about any of this. She had taken the deal because it was better than rotting in a cell. But now...

Now, it felt different.

"I guess... I didn't want to waste my life," she said quietly, her voice barely above a whisper. "I've made a lot of bad choices, and this felt like a chance to do something right."

Kael's eyes softened, just for a moment. "You don't seem like a bad person."

Liora huffed, a bitter laugh escaping her. "That's because you don't know me."

Kael opened his mouth to respond, but before he could say anything, the sound of footsteps echoed from outside the tower.

Liora shot to her feet, her heart pounding. "Did you hear that?"

Kael nodded, his expression darkening. "We're not alone."

Liora and Kael moved quickly to the entrance of the tower, pressing themselves against the stone walls, waiting. The footsteps grew louder, closer, until finally, a figure stepped into view.

It was a woman, tall and graceful, with pale skin and flowing, dark hair. Her eyes were the same icy blue as Kael's, and she moved with an eerie, dreamlike grace. Liora's breath caught in her throat. **She looked like Kael.**

The woman stepped into the light of the moon, her gaze sweeping over the crumbling tower as if searching for something.

Then, she spoke, her voice soft and haunting. "Kael? Where are you?"

Kael's body went rigid beside Liora. His face had gone pale, and his eyes were wide with shock.

Liora glanced at him, her pulse quickening. "Who is that?"

Kael's voice was barely audible. "My mother."

Liora's heart skipped a beat. **His mother?**

The woman's eyes flicked toward the tower, as if she could sense their presence. "Kael, please. Come back to me."

Liora turned to Kael, her voice urgent. "What's happening?"

Kael shook his head, his expression a mixture of confusion and fear. "I... I don't know. She's... she's been dead for years."

Liora swallowed hard, her pulse racing. "Then what is she doing here?"

Before Kael could respond, the woman's figure began to shift. Her skin paled further, her body becoming translucent, like a ghost fading into the mist. But her voice remained, soft and haunting, echoing through the dreamscape.

"Kael... you need to wake up..."

Kael's breath hitched, and he took a step forward, his hand reaching out toward the fading figure. But before he could touch her, she disappeared, dissolving into the air like smoke.

The silence that followed was deafening.

Liora turned to Kael, her heart still pounding. "Was that... real?"

Kael didn't answer. He just stared at the spot where the vision of his mother had stood, his eyes filled with a sadness that cut deeper than any curse.

The night was still, but the air felt charged, as if something terrible was about to happen. Liora could feel it—the thrum of magic in the air, the sharp edge of danger that seemed to hang over them.

Kael stood frozen, his eyes fixed on the spot where his mother had vanished, his face pale and drawn. Liora's heart ached for him, but there was no time to dwell on it. The shadows were stirring again, creeping closer, darker and more dangerous than before.

And then, it happened.

The ground beneath them trembled, and from the shadows, a figure emerged—a creature of pure darkness, its body twisting and shifting like smoke, its eyes glowing red with malice.

Liora's blood ran cold. **The Shadowthorn.**

The creature let out a low, guttural growl, its form rippling with dark magic. It moved toward them with terrifying speed, its shadowy limbs lashing out, seeking to tear them apart.

Kael reacted first, drawing a blade from the dreamscape itself, his eyes blazing with determination. But Liora could see the fear in his movements, the hesitation. He was still shaken from the vision.

"Kael, move!" she shouted, pushing him aside as the creature lunged at them.

Her hands flew up, and the thorns obeyed her call. They shot out from the ground, wrapping around the creature's limbs, pulling it back. But the Shadowthorn was powerful—too powerful. It tore through the thorns with ease, its growl turning into a roar of fury.

Liora's heart pounded as she pushed harder, calling every ounce of her magic to the surface. The thorns twisted and coiled, fighting against the darkness, but it wasn't enough.

The Shadowthorn broke free, its eyes locking onto Kael.

"No!" Liora screamed, throwing herself between them, her magic surging in one last desperate attempt to hold the creature back.

For a moment, time seemed to slow. The Shadowthorn lunged, and Liora felt the searing heat of its magic rushing toward her.

Then everything went dark.

CHAPTER 3
THE CURSE UNRAVELED

iora's senses returned slowly, as if she were rising from the depths of a dark sea. The world around her was fuzzy, her body heavy and numb. Her head throbbed, and she could taste blood in her mouth.

She blinked against the brightness, groaning as she tried to sit up. Her muscles screamed in protest, but she forced herself upright. She wasn't dead, which meant something had gone right. Or maybe wrong. She couldn't tell.

"Liora."

The voice was soft, filled with tension. She turned her head and found Kael kneeling beside her, his face pale, but alive. His dark hair hung in messy strands over his forehead, and his blue eyes were wide, full of something she couldn't quite place.

"You're awake," he said, as if he hadn't believed it would happen.

Liora tried to push herself up further, but Kael put a

firm hand on her shoulder, easing her back down. "Take it easy. You were out for a while."

"How long?" she asked, her voice coming out raspier than she'd expected.

Kael frowned. "I'm not sure. Time's... strange here. But it felt like hours."

Liora exhaled slowly, her head still spinning. She couldn't remember much after the attack, just the rush of magic and the cold, searing darkness of the Shadowthorn.

"How did we...?" she started, trailing off as she noticed the surroundings. They were no longer in the tower. They were outside, in a small, open clearing surrounded by trees. The air felt fresher here, calmer, as if the Dreamplane itself had softened around them.

Kael shifted, looking uncomfortable. "I dragged you out. After you collapsed, the Shadowthorn... retreated."

"Retreated?" Liora raised an eyebrow, her mind struggling to make sense of it. "Why? I thought it wanted to kill us."

Kael's jaw tightened. "I don't know. But I think it's not just after me anymore." His gaze flicked toward her, a hint of guilt in his eyes. "It's after both of us."

Liora winced, pulling herself into a sitting position despite Kael's protests. "Great. That's just what I needed."

They fell into silence, the weight of the Shadowthorn's threat settling between them. Liora rubbed her temples, trying to push the ache away. There was something Kael wasn't telling her, something more about the curse that he was keeping close to his chest.

"Kael," she said, her voice low, but firm. "What aren't you telling me?"

Kael's eyes flicked away, and for a moment, he didn't answer. The silence stretched on, thick with unspoken words. Finally, he sighed and sat down beside her, resting his arms on his knees.

"There's more to the curse than just the rose," he admitted, his voice quiet. "The Shadowthorn... it's not just a creature. It's tied to the magic of the Dreamplane. I don't know how, but I think it's feeding off the curse. Feeding off me."

Liora frowned, her mind racing. "You mean... it's getting stronger the longer you stay asleep?"

Kael nodded, his expression grim. "Yes. And now that you're here, it's started to feed off you, too."

Liora's stomach twisted. The thought of the Shadowthorn feeding on her, on Kael—it made her skin crawl. "So, what do we do? How do we stop it?"

Kael's gaze darkened. "We have to find the heart. That's the only way."

Liora felt a surge of frustration. "But we don't even know where it is! This place is a maze."

Kael's lips tightened. "I know. But there's something else. Something we haven't tried yet."

Liora narrowed her eyes. "What?"

Kael hesitated, then looked at her, his expression serious. "There are memories—pieces of my past—scattered throughout the Dreamplane. If we find them, we might be able to figure out how to unlock the heart."

Liora's eyebrows shot up. "Wait. You didn't mention that before."

"I wasn't sure if it would work," Kael admitted. "But after seeing my mother... that memory was real. And it gave me an idea. If we can piece together enough of my memories, we might find the answer."

Liora's mind whirled with the possibilities. It wasn't much, but it was something. And right now, something was better than nothing.

"Alright," she said, her voice steady. "Where do we start?"

The Dreamplane was quieter than it had been before, but the tension in the air hadn't lifted. Liora and Kael moved through the twisted woods, their footsteps muffled by the soft earth beneath them. The trees loomed tall and dark, their branches gnarled and twisted, reaching for the sky like crooked fingers.

The path ahead was barely visible, winding between the thick undergrowth and thorny vines. Liora's magic hummed at her fingertips, ready to spring to life at a moment's notice, but she kept it in check. She wasn't sure if the thorns here would obey her, or if they were connected to something darker—something that might fight back.

Kael walked beside her, his gaze fixed ahead, his expression tense. They hadn't spoken much since they left the clearing. The silence between them was thick, filled with unspoken thoughts. Liora could sense the weight of his memories pressing down on him, the fear of what they might uncover.

"Do you remember anything about this place?" Liora asked, her voice cutting through the quiet.

Kael shook his head, his jaw tight. "Not yet. But it feels familiar."

Liora nodded, though she wasn't sure how much that helped. The Dreamplane was vast, and everything here felt both familiar and foreign at the same time. It was a place built on memories, after all—both real and forgotten.

The path grew narrower as they ventured deeper into the forest, the trees closing in around them. The air felt thicker here, heavier, as if the very atmosphere was pressing down on them. Liora's skin prickled with unease.

Kael slowed his pace, his eyes narrowing as he scanned the trees. "Something's wrong."

Liora's heart skipped a beat. "What do you mean?"

Before Kael could answer, the ground beneath them shifted. Liora stumbled, her hands flying out to steady herself against a nearby tree. The earth trembled, and a deep, low rumble echoed through the forest.

"What—" Liora started, but her voice was cut off as the tree beside her began to move.

Her eyes widened as the tree's gnarled branches twisted and curled, bending toward her like the limbs of some great beast. The roots beneath her feet shifted, pulling free of the earth with a slow, creaking sound.

"Run!" Kael shouted, grabbing her arm and pulling her back as the tree lurched toward them.

They sprinted down the narrow path, dodging the twisted branches that reached out from all sides. The forest itself seemed to come alive, the trees groaning and shifting as if they were waking from some ancient slumber.

Liora's heart pounded in her chest as they raced through the undergrowth, the sound of cracking wood and

27

snapping branches filling the air. The forest wasn't just alive—it was hunting them.

They ran until they couldn't anymore, their breaths coming in ragged gasps. Liora's legs burned from the effort, and her lungs felt like they might explode, but she didn't dare stop until Kael pulled her into a small, hidden alcove in the side of a rock formation.

They pressed themselves into the narrow space, hearts pounding in their ears, waiting for the forest to settle.

After what felt like an eternity, the sounds of the moving trees faded, leaving them in an uneasy silence. Liora leaned against the cool stone, trying to catch her breath.

Kael's face was pale, his eyes wide with fear. "That's never happened before," he muttered, more to himself than to her.

"Yeah, well," Liora panted, resting her head against the wall, "first time for everything."

They sat there for a few minutes, letting the adrenaline fade. But even as the forest grew still again, the unease in Liora's chest didn't go away. She could feel it—something had changed. The Dreamplane was becoming more dangerous, more hostile.

Kael shifted beside her, his expression troubled. "We need to keep moving."

Liora didn't argue. She could feel the thorns pressing at the edges of her magic, restless and eager to respond. The

Dreamplane wasn't just reacting to Kael anymore. It was reacting to both of them.

As they climbed out of the alcove, Kael's gaze caught on something. He froze, his hand hovering in the air.

"What is it?" Liora asked, stepping closer.

Kael's eyes were fixed on a small, glowing object nestled in the roots of a nearby tree. It was faint, barely visible, but it pulsed with a soft, ethereal light.

Liora frowned. "What is that?"

Kael didn't answer. He stepped forward, his hand trembling as he reached for the glowing object. As his fingers brushed the light, the world around them seemed to shift. The air grew colder, and a strange sensation washed over Liora—a feeling of being pulled backward, into something deeper.

Suddenly, the forest disappeared, replaced by a swirling mist. The mist parted, revealing a scene from another time.

Liora watched in stunned silence as the memory unfolded before her.

It was Kael—only younger, barely a teenager. He stood in a grand hall, his face pale and tense, his hands clenched into fists at his sides. Before him stood a man—tall, imposing, with the same icy blue eyes as Kael. The resemblance was undeniable.

His father.

"I can't do this," Kael's younger voice echoed through the memory. "I'm not ready."

The man's face was hard, his eyes cold. "You have no choice, Kael. You are the prince. You must be strong."

"But—"

"There are no 'buts.' You will do your duty, or you will fail this kingdom."

Liora's chest tightened as she watched the scene unfold. She could see the fear in Kael's eyes, the way his shoulders hunched under the weight of his father's words.

The memory faded as quickly as it had appeared, leaving them standing once again in the silent forest.

Kael's hand dropped to his side, his face pale, his expression hollow. "That... was my father."

Liora didn't know what to say. The weight of the memory hung heavy between them, and she could see the pain in Kael's eyes, the burden he had carried for so long.

"He... he was a hard man," Kael said quietly, his voice barely audible. "He expected more from me than I could give."

Liora reached out, resting a hand on his arm. "You don't have to live up to him, you know."

Kael looked at her, his eyes filled with a mix of emotions—pain, fear, and something else. "But what if I do? What if that's the only way to break the curse?"

Liora shook her head, her voice firm. "We'll find another way."

———

The memory weighed on them both as they continued through the forest, but something had shifted between them. There was a new understanding in the silence, a quiet bond that hadn't been there before.

Kael led the way, his eyes scanning the twisted path ahead. The forest had grown quieter now, as if it were watching them, waiting for their next move. Liora kept close, her magic humming beneath her skin, ready to react at a moment's notice.

They walked in silence for what felt like hours, until finally, the trees began to thin, and the ground beneath their feet turned from soft earth to hard stone. Ahead of them, the forest opened up into a wide, barren clearing.

At the center of the clearing stood a single, massive stone structure—a doorway carved into the rock, its surface etched with strange, glowing symbols.

Kael slowed his pace, his eyes narrowing as he studied the doorway. "This is it."

Liora frowned. "It doesn't look like much."

"It's a gateway," Kael said quietly. "To the heart of the curse."

Liora's heart skipped a beat. "The heart? You mean... the rose?"

Kael nodded, his expression grim. "Yes. But it won't be easy to reach. There are... things guarding it."

Liora's pulse quickened, her mind racing. They were close now—so close to finding the heart and breaking the curse. But the thought of what might be waiting for them on the other side of that door filled her with a cold, gnawing dread.

"We need to be ready," Kael said, his voice tense. "Once we go through that door, there's no turning back."

Liora took a deep breath, her heart pounding in her chest. She could feel the weight of the curse pressing down on her, the shadow of the Shadowthorn lurking in the corners of her mind. But she wasn't about to back down now.

"I'm ready," she said, her voice steady.

Kael glanced at her, his expression softening. "Thank you. For coming this far."

Liora met his gaze, her heart skipping a beat. There was something in his eyes—something raw, unspoken, that made her chest tighten. For the first time, she felt like she wasn't just a tool in his fight against the curse. She was a partner. Maybe more.

"Don't thank me yet," she said, forcing a smile. "We're not done."

Kael's lips twitched into the faintest smile. "No, we're not."

Together, they stepped forward, toward the doorway and whatever waited on the other side.

The moment they crossed the threshold of the doorway, the world around them shifted again. The air grew colder, the light dimmer. Liora's skin prickled as they stepped into the darkness, her magic surging in response to the sudden change in atmosphere.

Kael walked beside her, his expression tense, his eyes scanning the shadows. The path ahead was narrow and winding, barely visible in the dim light. The walls around them were carved with strange, intricate patterns, glowing faintly with a cold, blue light.

"This is it," Kael said, his voice low. "The heart is close."

Liora's pulse quickened as they moved deeper into the passageway. The air felt thick with magic, heavy with the weight of the curse. She could feel it pressing down on her, pulling at her, as if the very air around her was trying to suffocate her.

The passageway opened up into a wide, circular chamber. At the center of the chamber stood a pedestal, and resting on the pedestal was a single, glowing rose. Its petals shimmered with a soft, ethereal light, casting a faint glow over the room.

Liora's heart skipped a beat. **The heart.**

Kael stepped forward, his eyes fixed on the rose. But as he reached out toward it, a low, rumbling growl echoed through the chamber.

Liora's blood ran cold as she turned to face the shadows. From the darkness, a figure emerged—a massive, hulking creature made of pure shadow, its eyes glowing red with malice.

The Shadowthorn.

Liora's breath caught in her throat as the creature lunged toward them, its massive, clawed hands reaching for Kael.

Without thinking, Liora threw herself between them, her magic surging to the surface. The thorns obeyed her call, wrapping around the creature's limbs, pulling it back. But the Shadowthorn was stronger this time—much stronger.

Kael shouted something, but the words were lost in the chaos. The Shadowthorn roared, tearing through the thorns with terrifying ease. It moved toward them again, its eyes burning with fury.

Liora's heart raced as she fought to hold the creature back, her magic straining under the pressure. But it wasn't enough. The Shadowthorn was too strong, too powerful.

Kael stepped forward, his eyes blazing with determination. "We have to break the curse. Now."

Liora's pulse quickened. "How?"

Kael's gaze flicked toward the rose, his expression grim. "The heart. We have to destroy it."

Liora's heart skipped a beat. **Destroy the heart?** But that would mean...

Before she could protest, Kael lunged toward the pedestal, his hand reaching for the rose. The Shadowthorn roared in fury, its claws slashing toward him.

"Kael, no!" Liora shouted, her voice echoing through the chamber.

But it was too late.

Kael's hand closed around the rose, and the world around them exploded into light.

CHAPTER 4
A HEART OF THORNS

Liora's vision blurred as the chamber exploded with light. The force of it sent her stumbling back, her body slamming hard against the cold stone floor. Her breath was knocked out of her chest, and for a moment, everything was noise and chaos.

When the light finally began to fade, Liora blinked, trying to steady herself. The room around her had changed. The dim, cold light that once filled the chamber was gone, replaced by an eerie red glow. The air felt thick, as if it were pulsing with energy, and the ground beneath her feet trembled.

Her heart pounded in her chest as she searched the chamber for Kael.

She found him near the pedestal, lying on the ground, his body still and lifeless.

"Kael!" Liora scrambled to her feet, her legs trembling as she rushed to his side. She dropped to her knees beside him, her hands shaking as she touched his shoulder.

He didn't move.

"Come on," she muttered, panic rising in her throat. "Don't do this. Wake up."

Her fingers pressed against his neck, searching for a pulse, but there was nothing—no movement, no breath. Just silence.

Liora's heart raced as she stared down at him, her chest tightening with fear. **This wasn't supposed to happen.** They had been so close. They were supposed to break the curse, not... not this.

"Kael!" she shouted, shaking him harder, but there was no response.

Her mind spun in a whirlwind of panic, her pulse pounding in her ears. She couldn't lose him. Not now. Not like this.

Tears pricked at the corners of her eyes, but before she could even process the emotions surging through her, the air in the room shifted. The red glow brightened, and the shadows along the walls began to ripple.

Liora's breath caught in her throat as she slowly turned her head.

The Shadowthorn was still there.

Its massive, hulking form loomed at the edge of the chamber, its red eyes glowing with a dark, malevolent light. The creature was watching her, its body rippling with shadow and magic, as if waiting for her to make a move.

For a brief, terrible moment, she was frozen. The weight of the Shadowthorn's presence pressed down on her, suffocating her, filling the room with its cold, dark energy.

But then something else happened. Something she hadn't expected.

Kael stirred.

His eyes fluttered open, and his chest rose with a sharp, ragged breath.

Liora gasped, relief washing over her so suddenly it almost knocked her back. "Kael!"

But Kael didn't seem to hear her. His eyes, now wide and unfocused, flicked toward the glowing rose still resting on the pedestal.

"The heart," he murmured, his voice faint. "It's still... whole."

Liora frowned, her pulse still racing in her chest. "But I thought—"

"The curse," Kael rasped, his voice a mix of pain and regret, "it's not just a spell placed on me. It's tied to my very essence. The Dreamplane was created centuries ago by my ancestors to protect the royal bloodline, binding it to the magic of the realm. But the curse warped that magic, turning it into a trap."

Liora's blood ran cold. "So destroying the heart means destroying... you?" Her voice shook at the realization.

Kael nodded, his face pale. "Yes. It was meant to ensure that no ruler could ever break the bond without... losing themselves. The curse ensures my connection to the Dreamplane is absolute."

Before she could finish, the Shadowthorn let out a low, rumbling growl, its body shifting as it moved closer. The red glow in the chamber pulsed with a sudden, violent intensity, and Liora's heart seized in her chest.

"Kael, we need to go," she urged, pulling him to his feet.

But Kael didn't move. His eyes were fixed on the rose, a deep sadness etched into his face. "I should have known…"

"Kael!" Liora snapped, shaking him. "We don't have time for this. We need to get out of here, now."

Kael finally tore his gaze from the rose, his eyes meeting hers. There was something broken in his expression—something that made Liora's chest ache in a way she didn't understand.

"We can't outrun it," he said quietly. "The curse is part of me now. No matter where we go, it'll follow."

Liora's breath caught in her throat, her mind spinning with the weight of his words. But before she could process it, the Shadowthorn roared.

The roar echoed through the chamber, shaking the walls and sending a pulse of dark energy through the air. Liora's heart leapt into her throat as the Shadowthorn lunged, its massive form barreling toward them with terrifying speed.

Without thinking, she grabbed Kael's arm and yanked him to his feet. He stumbled, his body still weak from the curse's hold, but he managed to stay upright.

"Run!" she shouted, her voice hoarse with panic.

They bolted toward the chamber's exit, their footsteps pounding against the stone floor as the Shadowthorn gave chase. The creature was faster than she'd expected, its shadowy form shifting and warping as it moved, closing the distance between them in seconds.

Liora's breath came in ragged gasps as she ran, her mind racing. They couldn't outrun it forever. The Shadowthorn would catch them eventually, and when it did...

She glanced over at Kael, his face pale and strained. He was barely holding himself together, his body still recovering from the explosion of magic. **He won't survive another attack.**

Liora's magic surged under her skin, her fingers twitching with the familiar pull of the thorns. She could feel them all around her, lurking just beneath the surface, waiting to be called. But she wasn't sure if they would be enough this time. The Shadowthorn was stronger than anything she had faced before.

As they rounded a corner, the Shadowthorn lunged again, its claws slashing toward them. Liora barely had time to react. She threw out her hand, and the thorns obeyed her call, snapping up from the ground and wrapping around the creature's limbs.

The Shadowthorn roared in fury, its massive body thrashing against the vines. Liora's heart pounded as she pushed harder, her magic straining under the pressure. But the creature was too strong. It tore through the thorns with terrifying ease, its glowing eyes locking onto them once more.

"We need to split up," Kael said suddenly, his voice breathless.

Liora's eyes widened in shock. "What? No!"

"It's after me," Kael insisted, his expression grim. "If I lead it away, you can get out. You can escape."

Liora's pulse quickened, her heart racing in her chest. "I'm not leaving you behind."

Kael's eyes softened, a sad smile tugging at his lips. "You don't have a choice."

Before Liora could argue, Kael pulled his arm free from her grip and bolted in the opposite direction, his footsteps echoing through the chamber.

The Shadowthorn let out a deafening roar and gave chase, its massive form barreling after him with terrifying speed.

Liora's heart leapt into her throat. **No.** She couldn't let him do this. She couldn't let him sacrifice himself for her. Not after everything they had been through.

Without thinking, she sprinted after them, her breath coming in ragged gasps. Her mind raced with panic, her magic surging wildly under her skin. **I won't let him die.**

The Shadowthorn was closing in on Kael, its claws outstretched, ready to strike. Liora's heart pounded as she pushed herself harder, faster, her magic boiling inside her.

And then, without thinking, she threw out her hand.

The thorns exploded from the ground, thicker and stronger than before, wrapping around the Shadowthorn's limbs and pulling it back with a violent snap. The creature roared in fury, its body thrashing against the vines, but this time, they held.

Liora's chest heaved as she stumbled to a stop, her body trembling with exhaustion. She could feel the strain of her magic, the pressure building under her skin, but she didn't care. She wouldn't let the Shadowthorn win.

Kael had stopped running, his eyes wide with shock as he turned to face her. "Liora—"

"Don't you dare run off again," she snapped, her voice trembling with emotion. "We're in this together, remember?"

Kael's expression softened, and for a moment, the tension between them seemed to fade. "I'm sorry," he said quietly.

Liora didn't answer. She was too exhausted to argue, too drained to care. All that mattered was that they were still alive.

For now.

They made it out of the chamber, but the fight had taken its toll. Liora's body ached, and her magic felt drained, like a well that had been emptied too many times. Kael wasn't much better—his face was pale, his eyes filled with exhaustion, and every step seemed to take more effort than the last.

They found a small alcove in the passageway and collapsed there, both of them too tired to move any further.

For a while, neither of them spoke. The air was thick with tension, but it wasn't the same as before. This time, it was heavier—charged with something unspoken, something that neither of them seemed ready to confront.

Kael was the first to break the silence. "I should have told you the truth about the heart."

Liora glanced at him, her chest tightening. "Why didn't you?"

Kael sighed, running a hand through his messy hair.

"Because I didn't want to believe it. I thought if we could destroy the heart, the curse would break. But it's not that simple."

Liora's brow furrowed. "What do you mean?"

"The heart," Kael said, his voice low, "isn't just the key to the curse. It's tied to my life force. If we destroy it... I die."

Liora's breath caught in her throat. She had suspected as much, but hearing him say it made her heart sink. "So, what do we do now?"

Kael was silent for a moment, his gaze distant. "There might be another way."

Liora's pulse quickened. "What?"

"The Shadowthorn," Kael said slowly, his voice tense. "It feeds on the curse. It's connected to it, and to me. If I can make a bargain with it, maybe we can break the curse without destroying the heart."

Liora's stomach twisted with dread. "A bargain? You're going to bargain with that thing?"

Kael's expression was grim. "It's the only chance we have."

Liora shook her head, her heart racing with panic. "No. There has to be another way. You can't—"

"I don't have a choice," Kael said quietly, his eyes meeting hers. "It's the only way to save both of us."

Liora's chest tightened. She could feel the weight of his words, the finality of the decision hanging over them. But she couldn't accept it. Not yet.

"There has to be another way," she insisted, her voice trembling.

Kael's eyes softened, and for a moment, the distance between them seemed to fade. "Liora..."

But before he could finish, the ground beneath them rumbled. The walls of the passageway shook, and the air grew thick with magic.

Liora's heart leapt into her throat. The Shadowthorn was coming.

The rumbling grew louder, and the walls trembled as the Shadowthorn's massive form emerged from the darkness, its eyes glowing red with fury. The creature let out a deafening roar, its body rippling with dark energy as it moved toward them.

Liora's heart raced as she scrambled to her feet, her magic flaring under her skin. She could feel the thorns pulsing beneath the surface, ready to respond to her call. But the Shadowthorn was stronger now—stronger than it had ever been.

Kael stood beside her, his face pale but determined. "We can't fight it like this."

Liora's breath came in ragged gasps as she tried to think of a plan. But before she could respond, Kael stepped forward, his eyes fixed on the creature.

"Kael, what are you—"

"I'm going to bargain with it," Kael said, his voice steady but filled with tension. "It's the only way."

Liora's heart pounded in her chest. "Kael, no!"

But Kael didn't stop. He took another step forward, his hand raised toward the creature. The Shadowthorn slowed its advance, its glowing eyes narrowing as it focused on him.

"Stop!" Liora shouted, her voice trembling with fear. "Don't do this!"

Kael glanced back at her, his expression filled with a sadness that cut deeper than any words. "It's the only way, Liora. I'm sorry."

Liora's breath caught in her throat, her chest tightening with a mix of fear and anger. She couldn't let him do this. She couldn't let him sacrifice himself for her.

Without thinking, she stepped forward, her magic surging to the surface. The thorns snapped to attention, wrapping around Kael's wrist, pulling him back.

"Liora—"

"No," she said, her voice firm. "We'll find another way. Together."

Kael's eyes softened, but before he could respond, the Shadowthorn let out a deafening roar. The creature lunged toward them, its massive form barreling forward with terrifying speed.

Liora's heart raced as she threw out her hand, the thorns obeying her call. They wrapped around the creature's limbs, pulling it back with a violent snap. The Shadowthorn roared in fury, its body thrashing against the vines, but this time, they held.

But it wasn't enough. The creature was too strong. It tore through the thorns, its glowing eyes locking onto Kael once more.

Liora's pulse quickened, her mind racing. They couldn't fight it like this. Not alone.

And then it hit her.

"We need to combine our magic," she said, her voice urgent.

Kael frowned, his brow furrowing. "What?"

"Your magic," Liora said quickly, her mind racing. "It's connected to the curse. If we combine it with mine, we might be able to overpower the Shadowthorn."

Just as they raised their hands, dark energy exploded between them, knocking Liora backward, her breath leaving her in a violent rush. The impact sent her crashing into the cold, twisted thorns of the Dreamplane, pinning her down.

"Liora!" Kael's voice echoed in the dark, but it sounded distant, muffled by the whirling magic in the air.

She struggled, her hands scratching at the thorny vines that bound her. Each move sent pain shooting through her body, but she had no time for pain. Through the fog of confusion, she saw Kael—his silhouette, standing alone, magic swirling violently around him.

"No," Liora gasped, panic seizing her. Kael was preparing for something. Something desperate.

She could feel the thorns in her blood react to the Dreamplane's magic, thrashing to life, but the dark vines around her squeezed tighter. Kael was about to offer himself. She had to reach him.

Her body trembled with the effort, but she pushed through, summoning the full force of her magic. The thorns beneath her skin exploded outward, snapping the dark vines with violent force.

"Kael, wait!"

With a final burst of energy, she reached him, her hand gripping his wrist just as his power surged, dark magic erupting from him like a wave.

Kael's eyes widened with realization. "But—"

"We don't have a choice," Liora said, her voice firm. "It's now or never."

Kael hesitated for a moment, then nodded, his expression grim. "Alright. Let's do this."

They stood side by side, their hands outstretched toward the Shadowthorn. Liora could feel the thorns surging beneath her skin, ready to respond to her call. Kael's magic hummed beside hers, dark and powerful, intertwined with the curse.

Together, they unleashed their magic.

The thorns exploded from the ground, wrapping around the Shadowthorn's massive form, pulling it back with a violent snap. Kael's magic surged through the air, dark tendrils of energy wrapping around the creature, binding it in place.

The Shadowthorn roared in fury, its body thrashing against the magic, but it was no use. The combined power of their magic was too strong.

With one final, deafening roar, the Shadowthorn shattered into a thousand pieces, dissolving into the air like smoke.

The chamber fell silent.

Liora's chest heaved as she lowered her hand, her body trembling with exhaustion. Kael stood beside her, his face pale but filled with relief.

"We did it," he said quietly, his voice filled with disbelief.

Liora's breath came in ragged gasps as she turned to face him. "Yeah. We did."

Kael's eyes softened, and for a moment, the tension between them seemed to fade. They stood there, side by side, in the quiet aftermath of the battle, their hearts still racing.

And in that moment, Liora realized something.

She wasn't just fighting for herself anymore.

She was fighting for him.

The chamber was quiet now, the air still and heavy with the aftermath of the battle. Liora's body ached, her magic drained, but the relief that flooded her chest was enough to keep her standing.

Kael stood beside her, his hand resting lightly on her arm. His face was pale, his eyes filled with a mixture of relief and exhaustion.

For a moment, neither of them spoke. The weight of the battle hung heavy between them, but so did something else—something unspoken, but undeniable.

"You saved me," Kael said quietly, his voice barely above a whisper.

Liora's chest tightened, her heart pounding in her chest. "We saved each other."

Kael's eyes softened, and for a moment, the distance between them seemed to fade. He took a step closer, his hand still resting on her arm.

"I don't deserve you," he said quietly, his voice filled with emotion.

Liora's breath caught in her throat. "That's not true."

Kael's eyes met hers, and for a moment, the world seemed to fade away. The Dreamplane, the curse, the Shadowthorn—it all disappeared, leaving only the two of them, standing in the quiet aftermath of everything they had fought for.

And in that moment, Liora knew.

She wasn't just here for herself.

She was here for him.

Kael took a step closer, his hand slipping from her arm to her hand, his fingers intertwining with hers. Liora's heart skipped a beat, her pulse quickening in her chest.

"Liora," Kael whispered, his voice filled with emotion.

Liora's breath hitched, her chest tightening as she looked up at him. There was something raw and real in his eyes, something that made her heart ache in a way she hadn't expected.

And then, without warning, he kissed her.

It wasn't desperate or frantic—it was slow, tentative, filled with all the emotion they had been holding back for so long. Liora's chest tightened as she kissed him back, her hand slipping up to cup his cheek.

For a moment, time seemed to stop. The world faded away, and all that existed was the two of them, standing in the quiet aftermath of everything they had fought for.

When they finally pulled apart, Kael's eyes were filled with something soft, something real.

"Thank you," he whispered, his voice barely audible.

Liora's heart pounded in her chest, her mind spinning with everything that had just happened. But as she looked up at him, a smile tugged at the corners of her lips.

"We're not done yet," she said quietly, her voice filled with determination.

Kael smiled softly, his hand still resting on hers. "No. We're not."

As their hands stretched out toward the Shadowthorn, Liora felt an unfamiliar pull—a resonance between her magic and the Dreamplane itself. The Dreamplane's energy, once distant, surged around her, amplifying her control over the thorns. It was as if the Dreamplane recognized her command, bending its rules to fit her will.

Beside her, Kael's magic flared. His power, which had always felt tethered to the curse, now pulsed with raw intensity. "The Dreamplane's feeding our magic," Kael said, his voice strained, "but it's unstable. Too much, and it could break us both."

Liora nodded, her chest tightening. "Then we have to use it carefully."

Together, they unleashed their power. The thorns erupted from the ground with greater force than ever before, coiling around the Shadowthorn's limbs. Kael's dark magic intertwined with hers, tendrils of energy binding the creature in place, but the ground trembled under their feet, as if the Dreamplane itself was protesting their interference.

CHAPTER 5

SHADOWS OF THE PAST

The quiet after the battle was unsettling. Liora could still feel the echo of the Shadowthorn's power in the air, lingering like a distant storm. The Dreamplane had fallen into an eerie stillness, the dark magic that had filled the air dissipating. But the curse still held them in its grip.

Kael stood by the pedestal, staring at the glowing rose —the heart of the curse. His fingers hovered over the delicate petals, but he didn't touch it. The tension in his body was palpable, and Liora could sense the turmoil churning beneath the surface.

She stepped up beside him, her hand resting gently on his arm. "We need to figure out what to do next," she said softly.

Kael's jaw tightened, but he nodded, his eyes still locked on the rose. "We're close, but... there's something I'm still not seeing. Something important."

Liora frowned, her eyes drifting over the rose's glow. The delicate flower seemed so harmless, but she knew better now. It held Kael's heart—and the key to his curse. But how could they break it without destroying him?

"What are we missing?" she murmured, half to herself.

Kael closed his eyes for a moment, his brow furrowing in concentration. "My memories. There's something hidden in them—something about the curse, about how it started. If we can find that last piece…"

Liora nodded. She had felt it, too, that nagging sense that they hadn't uncovered everything. The visions of Kael's past had given them clues, but there were still gaps —pieces of the puzzle they hadn't yet found.

"We'll find it," she said, her voice filled with quiet determination. "Whatever it is, we'll figure it out."

Kael's eyes flicked to hers, a glimmer of hope mingled with the weight of uncertainty. "I just hope we're not too late."

Liora swallowed hard. Time wasn't on their side—she could feel the curse tightening around them like a noose. But they couldn't afford to give up now.

"Let's start with the memories," she said, pulling her thoughts together. "There must be another fragment hidden somewhere in the Dreamplane."

Kael hesitated, then nodded. "There's one place we haven't searched yet."

The landscape of the Dreamplane shifted again as they made their way through the twisted forest and into a vast, crumbling ruin. The towering stone walls were covered in moss and vines, the remnants of a forgotten palace that seemed to stretch endlessly into the distance. Liora could feel the weight of history pressing down on her as they entered, the air thick with the echoes of a past long buried.

Kael walked ahead, his footsteps echoing against the stone. His expression was distant, his eyes scanning the ruins as if searching for something he couldn't quite see.

"This place..." he murmured, his voice barely audible. "It feels familiar."

Liora frowned, glancing around. The ruins were ancient, overgrown with the passage of time. But there was something hauntingly beautiful about them—a sense of grandeur that had been lost to decay.

"You think this is another memory?" she asked, her voice low.

Kael nodded slowly. "It's more than that. I think this place is important... to the curse."

They moved deeper into the ruins, passing through crumbling archways and shattered courtyards. The air grew colder the further they went, the shadows lengthening with each step. Liora's magic hummed under her skin, the thorns pulsing with a faint energy, as if they were reacting to the place.

As they entered what appeared to be a grand hall, Kael stopped suddenly, his body tensing.

Liora followed his gaze—and froze.

At the center of the hall, surrounded by broken pillars and scattered debris, stood a single figure.

It was Kael.

Or at least, a memory of him.

Liora's breath caught in her throat as she watched the younger version of Kael move through the hall, his expression tense and determined. He was dressed in royal garb, his posture rigid, as if preparing for something important.

The vision shifted, and another figure appeared—a man with sharp features and cold eyes. Liora recognized him immediately. It was Kael's father, the same man they had seen in the earlier memory.

The two figures stood facing each other, their gazes locked in a tense standoff.

"You've failed me again," the older man said, his voice hard as steel.

Young Kael's fists clenched at his sides, his jaw tight with suppressed emotion. "I'm trying. But the curse—"

"You're not trying hard enough," his father snapped, cutting him off. "You've had every opportunity to succeed, and yet here we are, no closer to breaking the curse than when it began."

Kael's face twisted with frustration. "I don't even know how it started! How can I break it if I don't understand it?"

His father's gaze darkened, his eyes narrowing. "You're weak, Kael. Too weak to do what's necessary."

The younger Kael took a step forward, his voice trembling with anger. "What are you talking about?"

The vision blurred, and the figure of Kael's father leaned in, his voice a low, menacing whisper. "You should never have been born."

Liora's blood ran cold.

The vision shattered.

Kael stood frozen in place, his face pale, his eyes wide with shock. Liora reached out, her hand brushing his arm. "Kael…"

But he didn't respond. He was staring at the spot where

the vision had just played out, his expression filled with disbelief.

"He knew," Kael whispered, his voice hollow. "My father knew about the curse. He knew the whole time."

Liora's chest tightened. "How? Why didn't he tell you?"

Kael shook his head, his hands trembling at his sides. "Because he didn't want me to break it. He didn't want me to succeed."

Liora's breath caught in her throat. "But why not?"

Kael's eyes filled with a dark realization, his voice barely audible. "Because the curse is tied to me. It was meant to keep me in check... to control me."

The weight of his words hung heavy in the air, and Liora could feel the truth sinking in. The curse wasn't just some random spell—it had been placed on Kael deliberately, to bind him, to weaken him.

Liora's stomach twisted with anger. "Your father did this to you?"

Kael's eyes darkened, his jaw clenched with barely suppressed rage. "He didn't care about me. He only cared about his legacy. And if I broke the curse, I would have more power than he ever did. He couldn't risk that."

Liora's pulse raced, her mind reeling with the weight of the revelation. It made sense now—why the curse had always felt so personal, so deeply connected to Kael's life. His father had used it as a weapon, a way to keep him under control.

"We can still break it," Liora said, her voice filled with quiet determination. "We'll find a way."

Kael's eyes flicked to hers, and for a moment, the raw

vulnerability in his gaze made her heart ache. "I don't know if I can do this, Liora."

Liora stepped closer, her hand resting on his arm. "You don't have to do it alone. We'll figure it out. Together."

Kael's gaze softened, and for a moment, the distance between them seemed to fade. "Thank you," he whispered, his voice barely audible.

Liora's heart pounded in her chest, but before she could respond, a faint sound echoed through the ruins—a low, distant rumble, like the growl of a storm.

They weren't alone.

The rumble grew louder, reverberating through the crumbling walls of the ancient palace. Liora's pulse quickened as she turned, her eyes scanning the shadows that clung to the edges of the hall.

"What was that?" she whispered, her voice tense.

Kael's body stiffened beside her, his gaze sharp and focused. "I don't know. But we need to move."

Liora nodded, her magic already humming under her skin. The thorns were restless, pulsing with energy, as if sensing the danger that lurked nearby. She could feel it, too—a dark presence, like the Shadowthorn, but different. It was quieter, more insidious.

They moved quickly through the ruins, their footsteps echoing against the stone. The air grew colder, the shadows deepening as they descended into the lower levels of the palace. Liora's heart raced with every step, her senses on high alert.

As they rounded a corner, the rumble grew louder, shaking the ground beneath their feet.

And then, from the darkness, a figure emerged.

Liora's breath caught in her throat.

The figure was tall and cloaked in shadow, its face obscured by a hood that seemed to shift and ripple with dark energy. Its eyes glowed faintly from beneath the hood, red and malevolent, like the Shadowthorn's, but far more dangerous.

Liora's chest tightened with fear as she instinctively stepped in front of Kael, her magic flaring to the surface.

The figure spoke, its voice a low, eerie hiss that sent chills down her spine. "You've come far, but you'll go no further."

Kael's eyes narrowed, his body tense. "Who are you?"

The figure didn't respond. Instead, it took a step closer, its presence radiating dark magic. The air around them crackled with tension, and Liora could feel the thorns pulsing beneath her skin, ready to respond.

But before she could act, the figure raised its hand, and the ground beneath them shook violently.

Liora stumbled, her magic flaring wildly as the ruins around them began to collapse. Stone pillars crumbled, and the ceiling groaned under the weight of the destruction.

"We need to go!" Kael shouted, grabbing her arm.

Liora's heart pounded as they bolted down the narrow passageway, the walls shaking with every step. The figure's laughter echoed behind them, dark and sinister, as the ground continued to rumble.

They raced through the ruins, dodging falling debris

and crumbling stone. Liora's magic surged under her skin, the thorns snapping to attention as they moved, but it wasn't enough to stop the destruction. The figure's power was too strong, too overwhelming.

As they reached the exit, the passageway collapsed behind them, sealing them off from the shadowy figure.

For a moment, the world was silent.

Liora's breath came in ragged gasps as she leaned against the wall, her heart pounding in her chest. Kael stood beside her, his face pale but determined.

"That was... something new," Liora muttered, still catching her breath.

Kael's brow furrowed, his expression tense. "It wasn't the Shadowthorn. It was something else—something worse."

Liora's stomach twisted with unease. The Shadowthorn had been terrifying, but this new enemy felt even more dangerous. She could still feel its dark presence lingering in the air, like a storm waiting to strike.

"We need to figure out what it wants," she said, her voice steady despite the fear gnawing at her insides. "Before it comes after us again."

Kael nodded, his jaw tight. "We need to hurry. The curse is weakening, but the Dreamplane is becoming more unstable. If we don't act fast, we could lose everything."

Liora's pulse quickened. She knew he was right. Time was running out.

As they moved further away from the ruins, the air grew thicker, the landscape shifting in strange, unnatural ways. The Dreamplane was becoming more unpredictable, more dangerous. Liora could feel it pressing down on her, like a weight she couldn't shake.

Kael walked beside her, his expression tense and focused. The encounter with the shadowy figure had left them both on edge, but Liora could sense something else weighing on him—something deeper.

They came to a stop near a quiet, hidden alcove, the air around them humming with magic. Liora leaned against a tree, her body still aching from the earlier battle, but her mind racing with thoughts.

Kael stood in front of her, his eyes distant. He hadn't said much since the collapse, but Liora knew there was something he wasn't telling her.

"Kael," she said quietly, her voice breaking the silence. "What's going on?"

Kael's eyes flicked to hers, and for a moment, the weight of everything they had been through seemed to crash down on him. His shoulders slumped, and he let out a long, ragged breath.

"There's something I haven't told you," he admitted, his voice low. "Something about the curse."

Liora's heart skipped a beat. "What is it?"

Kael hesitated, his gaze flicking away. "The Dreamplane's magic..." Kael's voice faltered, his words heavy with something unspoken. He didn't look at her, his eyes fixed on the dark woods in the distance. "It's... not just about me."

Liora felt a shift in the air between them, a coldness that made her spine stiffen. "Kael... what do you mean?"

He let out a breath that was almost a sigh, but there was no relief in it. "If we destroy the curse... the Dreamplane won't survive," Kael said, his voice thick with the weight of centuries-old magic. "The Dreamplane is more than just a place in my mind, Liora. It's connected to the balance of magic across the kingdom. My ancestors tied it to the flow of magical energy that sustains Solstraea's defenses. If it collapses, the magical protections on the kingdom will crumble with it."

Liora stared at him, the weight of his words hitting her like a blow. "You're saying the entire kingdom is bound to the Dreamplane? And if it falls, the kingdom—"

Kael nodded, his expression grim. "Everything will unravel."

Kael's jaw clenched, and he finally turned to meet her gaze. His eyes were shadowed, filled with an old fear. "It's all connected, Liora. Every last part of it."

Liora's heart pounded in her chest, her mind spinning with the weight of his words. The Dreamplane was the key to breaking the curse, but if it fell apart in the process, they could lose everything—Kael, the kingdom, even their own lives.

"We'll figure something out," she said, her voice filled with determination. "There has to be a way to break the curse without destroying the Dreamplane."

Kael's eyes softened, but there was still a shadow of doubt in his gaze. "I hope you're right."

Liora reached out, her hand brushing his arm. "We'll find a way. I'm not giving up on you."

Kael's breath hitched, and for a moment, the distance between them seemed to dissolve. He stepped closer, his eyes searching hers, as if looking for reassurance, for hope.

Liora's heart pounded in her chest, but she didn't look away.

"I don't deserve you," Kael whispered, his voice barely audible.

Liora's chest tightened, her breath catching in her throat. "You do."

Before she could say anything more, Kael closed the distance between them, his lips brushing hers in a soft, tentative kiss.

It wasn't frantic or desperate—just slow, filled with the weight of everything they had been through. Liora's heart raced as she kissed him back, her hand slipping up to cup his cheek.

When they finally pulled apart, Kael's eyes were filled with something raw, something real.

"We'll find a way," he whispered, his voice filled with quiet determination.

Liora smiled, her chest tight with emotion. "Together."

With renewed determination, they pressed on, their focus now fully on finding the last piece of the puzzle. The Dreamplane continued to shift around them, the magic growing more unstable with every step, but Liora and Kael didn't slow down. They couldn't afford to.

Finally, after what felt like hours of searching, they reached the edge of a cliff that overlooked a vast, swirling abyss. The air here was thick with magic, the ground trembling beneath their feet.

Liora's pulse quickened as she stared down into the darkness. "This is it, isn't it?"

Kael nodded, his eyes fixed on the abyss. "The last memory. It's down there."

Liora's heart pounded in her chest as they stood on the edge of the cliff, the weight of everything they had been through pressing down on her. This was their final chance —the last piece of the puzzle they needed to break the curse.

Kael took a deep breath, his eyes filled with determination. "Let's finish this."

Together, they stepped forward, their hands intertwined as they plunged into the darkness below.

CHAPTER 6
THE HEART OF THE CURSE

The plunge into the abyss was like falling through a dream within a dream—endless, weightless, and terrifying. Liora's heart pounded in her chest as the world around them blurred into darkness. She held tightly to Kael's hand, the only anchor in the swirling void.

For a moment, there was nothing but silence. The air was cold, thick with magic and memory, and Liora couldn't tell if they were still falling or if time itself had stopped. The only thing she knew for certain was that they were going deeper—into the heart of the Dreamplane, into the very core of the curse.

Her pulse quickened, her magic humming under her skin, restless and ready. She could feel the thorns stirring, sensing the danger that lurked just beneath the surface. The abyss wasn't just empty—it was alive, filled with shadows and echoes of the past.

And then, with a sudden jolt, they landed.

The impact knocked the breath from Liora's lungs, but

she managed to stay on her feet, her fingers still tightly intertwined with Kael's. The ground beneath them was cold, solid, but it didn't feel real. It was like standing on the edge of a memory—half-formed, fragile, as if one wrong step could send them plunging back into the void.

Liora's breath came in ragged gasps as she glanced around. They were standing in a vast, empty landscape, surrounded by darkness. The only light came from the faint, ethereal glow that seemed to radiate from the ground itself, casting strange shadows that danced at the edges of her vision.

"This place..." Kael murmured, his voice barely audible. "I know this place."

Liora turned to him, her heart skipping a beat. "What is it?"

Kael's brow furrowed, his eyes distant, as if he were seeing something she couldn't. "It's... the beginning. The place where the curse was born."

Liora's chest tightened. "Then this is where we end it."

Kael's gaze flicked to hers, and for a moment, the weight of everything they had been through seemed to settle between them. He nodded, his jaw tight with determination. "Yes."

Together, they took a step forward, the ground beneath them pulsing with energy. As they moved deeper into the abyss, the darkness began to shift, swirling like mist, until finally, a shape began to emerge.

At the center of the abyss, surrounded by a ring of glowing thorns, stood a figure.

Liora's breath caught in her throat.

It was Kael.

Or rather, a version of him—an echo of his past, frozen in time. He was younger, his face pale and strained, his eyes filled with a fear that Liora had never seen before. His gaze fixed on something just beyond the circle of thorns.

Liora's pulse quickened as they approached the figure, her magic surging under her skin. She could feel the power radiating from the thorns, pulsing with dark energy. The air around them crackled with tension, and she knew that they were standing on the edge of something dangerous—something that had been waiting for them.

Kael took a step closer, his hand tightening around hers. "This is the memory," he said quietly, his voice filled with awe and fear. "This is where it all started."

Liora's chest tightened. "What happens next?"

Kael's eyes flicked to the figure, his expression tense. "I... I don't know."

And then, before they could take another step, the memory began to shift.

The echo of Kael moved, his body turning toward the darkness. The shadows swirled, and from the mist, a second figure appeared—a man with cold, sharp features and eyes that glowed faintly with dark magic.

Liora's blood ran cold. *Kael's father.*

The two figures stood facing each other, the air between them crackling with magic. Liora could feel the weight of it pressing down on her, suffocating her. This wasn't just a memory—it was a moment of power, of destruction, of betrayal.

The older man's voice echoed through the abyss, filled with venom. "You were never meant to be king."

Kael's younger self recoiled, his face pale with fear. "But the curse—"

"The curse is your punishment," his father snarled, his eyes blazing with hatred. "You are a failure, Kael. A weak, pathetic child who will never rule this kingdom."

The words struck like a physical blow, and Liora could feel the weight of them, the pain they carried. Her heart ached for the boy Kael had been, for the cruelty he had endured at the hands of his father.

But the memory wasn't over.

The older man raised his hand, dark magic swirling around him. "You will never be free. You will never be anything."

And with a flick of his wrist, the curse was born.

The dark magic surged forward, wrapping around the younger Kael, pulling him into the darkness. The air crackled with energy, the ground trembling beneath their feet as the curse took hold, binding Kael to the Dreamplane, to the heart of the rose.

Liora's breath caught in her throat as the memory played out before them. She could feel the raw power of the curse, the way it had twisted and warped over the years, feeding on Kael's fear, his doubt, his pain.

And then, just as suddenly as it had begun, the memory shattered.

The figures disappeared, and the darkness closed in around them once more.

Kael stood frozen beside her, his body trembling with the weight of what they had just seen.

"He did this to me," Kael whispered, his voice hollow. "My own father cursed me."

Liora's heart ached as she turned to him, her hand resting on his arm. "Kael…"

But before she could say anything more, the air around them shifted again.

The curse wasn't finished with them yet.

———

The darkness rippled, and from the shadows, the figure of Kael's father reappeared. But this time, he wasn't just a memory—he was something more. His body was cloaked in shadow, his eyes glowing red with the same malevolent light as the Shadowthorn.

Liora's pulse quickened, her magic flaring under her skin. She could feel the thorns pulsing beneath the surface, ready to respond, but there was something different about this figure—something far more dangerous.

Kael's body tensed beside her, his eyes wide with shock. "It's him."

Liora's chest tightened. "Your father?"

Kael's gaze was fixed on the figure, his voice filled with disbelief. "It's not just a memory. It's… him."

The figure stepped forward, the shadows swirling around him like smoke. His voice was cold, filled with contempt. "You thought you could escape me, Kael? You thought you could break the curse?"

Liora's breath caught in her throat. **This wasn't just a memory. It was the curse itself—alive, sentient, and filled with hatred.**

Kael took a step back, his body trembling with fear.

"You're not real. You're just... you're just a piece of the curse."

The figure's lips curled into a cruel smile. "Am I? Or am I the part of you that you've always feared—the part that will never be free?"

Liora's heart raced as the figure moved closer, its eyes burning with malevolent light. She could feel the weight of the curse pressing down on them, suffocating them. The air crackled with dark magic, and Liora knew they were standing on the edge of a battle they might not survive.

"We can break the curse," Liora said, her voice steady despite the fear gnawing at her insides. "We know the truth now."

The figure's gaze flicked to hers, its smile widening. "You think you've won, little girl? The curse isn't something you can just break. It's part of Kael. It's part of who he is."

Liora's chest tightened, but she didn't back down. "That's not true. The curse was forced on him. It doesn't define him."

The figure let out a low, dark laugh. "You're a fool."

Before Liora could respond, a deafening crack split the air as the figure lunged, the darkness swirling like a living storm. Its energy was raw, feral—wild magic that lashed at them both. The force of it knocked Liora back, the thorns at her fingertips trembling under the pressure.

Kael reacted first, his magic flaring to life as he threw out his hand. Dark tendrils of energy shot forward, wrapping around the figure, holding it in place.

But it wasn't enough.

The figure roared, tearing through the magic with terrifying ease. Its glowing eyes locked onto Kael, its body shifting as it moved toward him, its hands outstretched.

Liora's heart leapt into her throat as she threw herself between them, her magic surging to the surface. The thorns snapped to attention, wrapping around the figure's limbs, pulling it back with a violent snap.

But the figure didn't stop.

It tore through the thorns, its eyes blazing with fury as it lunged toward Kael again.

"Liora," Kael's voice was tight, eyes glinting with desperation, "It's the core of the curse. We destroy it—or we lose everything."

Liora's breath came in ragged gasps as she fought to hold the figure back. "How?"

Kael's eyes flicked to hers, his expression grim. "We have to destroy the heart."

Liora's blood ran cold. "But that means—"

Kael's gaze softened, his voice filled with quiet resolve. "I know what this means," Kael's words were a whisper, but they carried the weight of an impossible decision. "If it's the only way... then we do it. Even if..." his voice broke, eyes pleading with her for strength.

Liora's heart pounded in her chest, her mind racing. **Destroy the heart?** But that would mean losing Kael. She couldn't do that. She couldn't lose him—not now.

But before she could respond, the figure let out a deafening roar, its body surging forward with terrifying speed.

Liora's magic flared, the thorns snapping to attention as she threw herself between the figure and Kael. She could feel the weight of the curse pressing down on her, suffocating her, but she didn't back down.

She wouldn't let the curse win.

The battle was chaotic. Liora's magic surged wildly, the thorns wrapping around the figure again and again, but each time, the creature tore through them with terrifying ease. Kael fought beside her, his dark magic crackling through the air, but the figure was relentless.

"We can't hold it off much longer," Kael shouted, his voice strained.

Liora's heart pounded in her chest. She knew he was right. The figure was too strong, too powerful. They couldn't win this battle by force alone.

Her eyes flicked to the heart of the rose, still glowing faintly in the distance. The answer was there—she knew it was. But how could they destroy it without destroying Kael?

And then, in the chaos of the fight, an idea struck her.

Liora's breath caught in her throat as she turned to Kael, her voice trembling with urgency. "We don't have to destroy it. We just have to change it."

Kael's eyes widened, his magic faltering for a moment. "What?"

"The heart—it's tied to the curse, but it's also tied to you," Liora said quickly, her mind racing. "If we use our magic together, we might be able to rewrite it. Change the curse, turn it into something else."

Kael's gaze flicked to the heart, his expression filled with doubt. "But what if it doesn't work?"

Liora's chest tightened, her heart pounding in her chest. "We don't have another choice."

Kael hesitated for a moment, then nodded, his jaw tight with determination. "Alright. Let's do it."

Together, they turned toward the heart of the rose, their hands outstretched. Liora could feel the thorns pulsing beneath her skin, the magic swirling inside her, ready to respond.

Kael's dark magic flared beside hers, crackling with energy.

And then, with one final, desperate surge of power, they unleashed their magic.

The thorns wrapped around the heart, intertwining with Kael's dark energy. The air around them crackled with magic, the ground trembling beneath their feet as the curse fought back.

The figure let out a deafening roar, its body writhing in agony as the magic surged through the Dreamplane, tearing at the fabric of the curse.

Liora's heart pounded as she pushed harder, her magic straining under the pressure. She could feel the curse unraveling, the dark magic twisting and warping, but it wasn't enough.

"We need more!" Kael shouted, his voice filled with desperation.

Liora's breath came in ragged gasps as she poured everything she had into the spell, her body trembling with the effort. The thorns tightened around the heart, squeezing the last remnants of the curse.

And then, with a sudden, blinding flash of light, the heart shattered.

The figure let out one final, agonized scream before dissolving into nothingness.

The curse was broken.

The world around them was still. The Dreamplane, once filled with dark magic and shadows, had fallen into a strange, quiet calm. The air was thick with the remnants of the curse, but Liora could feel the difference—the weight had lifted, the darkness had faded.

But something was wrong.

Kael stood beside her, his body tense, his eyes wide with shock. His hands were trembling, and when Liora looked at him, her heart dropped.

His face was pale—too pale.

"Kael," she whispered, her voice trembling with fear. "What's happening?"

Kael's gaze flicked to hers, filled with a deep, quiet sadness. "The curse is broken. But…"

Liora's breath caught in her throat. "But what?"

Kael took a step back, his body swaying slightly. "I was tied to the curse, Liora. And now that it's gone…"

Liora's heart pounded in her chest, panic rising in her throat. "No. No, we changed it. We fixed it. You're supposed to be free."

Kael's lips twitched into a sad smile. "I am. But there's always a price."

Liora's chest tightened as she reached out, grabbing his arm. "No. You can't leave me. Not now."

Kael's gaze softened, his eyes filled with a deep, raw

emotion. "I'm sorry."

Liora's breath came in ragged gasps, her mind spinning with the weight of what was happening. This wasn't how it was supposed to end. They had broken the curse. They were supposed to be free—together.

But Kael was fading, slipping away with the remnants of the curse.

"Kael, please," she whispered, her voice breaking. "Don't leave me."

Kael's hand slipped into hers, his fingers intertwining with hers one last time. "You saved me, Liora. You gave me something I never thought I could have."

Liora's chest tightened, her heart shattering with every word. "I can't do this without you."

Kael's gaze held hers, filled with a quiet, bittersweet sadness. "You don't have to. I'll always be with you."

And then, with one final, whispered breath, Kael disappeared.

Liora stood frozen, her hand still outstretched, her heart aching with a grief so deep it felt like it might swallow her whole.

Kael was gone.

Time passed, though Liora couldn't tell how long. The Dreamplane had fallen into a deep, quiet stillness, the magic that once filled the air now gone. But despite the calm, the weight of Kael's absence pressed down on her, suffocating her.

She had saved him—broken the curse—but it hadn't

been enough. Kael was gone, and the emptiness left in his wake was almost too much to bear.

But then, as she stood in the quiet aftermath, something stirred.

The rose.

Liora's breath caught in her throat as she turned toward the heart of the rose, still glowing faintly in the dim light of the Dreamplane. It had shattered during the battle, but now... it was reforming.

The petals, once delicate and fragile, were knitting themselves back together, glowing with a soft, ethereal light. The magic that had once bound Kael to the curse had changed, transformed into something new.

Liora's heart pounded in her chest as she reached out, her fingers brushing the edge of the newly formed rose.

And then, from the soft glow of the petals, a figure appeared.

Liora's breath caught in her throat.

Kael.

He stood before her, his body whole, his eyes filled with life and light. The curse was gone, the darkness that had once haunted him now replaced with something pure, something real.

"Kael," Liora whispered, her voice trembling with disbelief. "You're alive."

Kael's lips twitched into a soft, relieved smile. "I told you I'd always be with you."

Liora's heart raced as she stepped forward, her hand reaching out to touch his. The warmth of his skin was real, the steady beat of his pulse beneath her fingers proof that he was truly alive.

Tears welled in her eyes as she threw her arms around him, pulling him close. Kael held her tightly, his breath warm against her hair, and for the first time, the weight of the curse, the danger, the fear—it all melted away.

They had won.

The curse was broken, and they were free.

Together.

CHAPTER 7
A NEW DAWN

T he first thing Liora noticed when they returned to the waking world was the light.

It was warm, golden, and pure—so different from the cold, shadow-filled Dreamplane they had left behind. The air was fresh, filled with the scent of blooming flowers, and the soft chirping of birds echoed from the distant trees.

For a moment, Liora just stood there, taking it all in. She hadn't realized how much she had missed the real world—the simple beauty of it. The Dreamplane had been a place of shifting darkness and fragile memories, but here, everything was solid, certain.

Beside her, Kael stood quietly, his eyes scanning the familiar landscape of the royal gardens. There was a faint breeze that tugged at his dark hair, and his face, no longer marked by the curse's shadow, looked peaceful in the morning light.

Liora's heart fluttered at the sight of him. After everything they had been through, after all the battles they had fought and the sacrifices they had made, he was here. He was alive.

"You're staring," Kael said softly, a faint smile tugging at the corners of his lips.

Liora blinked, feeling a blush rise to her cheeks. "I was just... making sure you're real."

Kael's smile widened, his eyes warm. "I'm real. I promise."

Liora's chest tightened with emotion, but before she could respond, the sound of footsteps drew their attention. They turned to see a group of people approaching—royal guards, dressed in their pristine armor, and among them, a woman with sharp eyes and a confident stride.

Callia.

The mage stopped in front of them, her gaze sweeping over Kael before settling on Liora. There was a flicker of surprise in her expression, quickly replaced by something softer—something almost like pride.

"You did it," Callia said quietly, her voice filled with a strange mix of awe and disbelief. "You broke the curse."

Liora nodded, her heart still racing with the weight of everything they had accomplished. "We did."

Callia's eyes flicked to Kael, and for a moment, the air between them was heavy with unspoken words. Then, she inclined her head, her tone respectful. "Your Highness."

Kael shifted, a faint shadow of uncertainty passing over his face. "I... I'm not sure I deserve that title anymore."

Callia raised an eyebrow. "The people of Solstraea need a king. And you are still the rightful heir."

Kael's lips pressed into a thin line, his eyes dark with thought. Liora could see the conflict in him—the weight of the crown he had once been meant to wear, and the fear that he might not be worthy of it.

But then, Kael's gaze shifted to Liora, and something in his expression softened.

"I won't be a king like my father," Kael said quietly, his voice filled with quiet determination. "I'll be better."

Liora's heart swelled with pride. She knew Kael had struggled with his past, with the legacy of his father's cruelty, but she also knew that he was different. He wasn't defined by the mistakes of those who came before him.

Callia gave a small, approving nod. "Then I believe Solstraea will be in good hands."

The return to the palace was bittersweet.

As Kael and Liora passed through the gates, the royal guards saluted, their expressions filled with a mixture of awe and respect. The news of the prince's awakening had spread quickly through the kingdom, and now, people gathered in the streets, whispering in hushed tones as they watched their future king walk among them.

But for Kael, the weight of the crown was already pressing down on him.

Liora could see it in the way his shoulders tensed, the way his gaze flicked nervously toward the grand towers of the palace. The responsibilities of ruling had once been far from his mind, trapped as he had been in the Dreamplane, but now they loomed large and unavoidable.

As they entered the throne room, the vast hall echoed with silence. Sunlight streamed through the high windows, casting long shadows across the floor. The throne, a grand and imposing structure of gold and marble, sat at the far end of the room, empty and waiting.

Kael hesitated at the entrance, his eyes fixed on the throne.

Liora's heart ached as she watched him. She could see the doubt in his expression, the fear that he wouldn't live up to the expectations placed on him.

"You don't have to do this alone," Liora said softly, stepping closer to him.

Kael turned to her, his eyes filled with a mix of gratitude and vulnerability. "I know. But I can't help feeling... like I'm not ready."

Liora reached out, her hand resting gently on his arm. "No one's ever really ready. But that doesn't mean you're not capable."

Kael's gaze softened, his lips twitching into a faint smile. "What would I do without you?"

Liora smirked, her heart lighter for a moment. "Fall apart, probably."

Kael laughed softly, but the sound was tinged with a note of tension. His eyes flicked back to the throne, his expression turning serious once more. "I just... I don't want to be like him."

"You won't be," Liora said firmly. "You're not your father, Kael. You're better than he is. You care about people. You want to do what's right."

Kael's eyes met hers, filled with a raw, quiet intensity. "I hope you're right."

Liora smiled softly, her fingers tightening around his arm. "I know I am."

For a moment, they stood in silence, the weight of the future pressing down on both of them. But then, with a deep breath, Kael straightened his shoulders, his expression hardening with resolve.

"I'll do it," he said quietly, his voice steady. "For the kingdom. For the people."

Liora's heart swelled with pride as she nodded, her chest tight with emotion. "And I'll be right here with you. Whatever happens."

Kael's gaze softened, and for a moment, the distance between them seemed to disappear. He reached out, his fingers brushing hers, and Liora's heart skipped a beat.

"Thank you," he whispered, his voice filled with quiet sincerity.

Liora smiled, her heart full. "You don't have to thank me. We're in this together."

Later that evening, after the formalities of Kael's return had settled, Liora found herself standing on one of the palace balconies, gazing out over the sprawling city of Solstraea. The sun was beginning to set, casting the sky in hues of pink and gold, and the gentle breeze carried the distant sounds of life—people celebrating, talking, laughing.

But Liora's mind was elsewhere.

She thought about everything that had happened—the curse, the battles, the revelations. She had come to the palace as a thief, a girl with no future, no hope of redemption. And now, she stood beside the prince of Solstraea, her heart full of things she had never expected to feel.

It was almost too much to take in.

"You're thinking too hard again."

Kael's voice broke through her thoughts, and Liora turned to see him standing behind her, a soft smile playing on his lips. He stepped onto the balcony, joining her at the railing, his eyes following her gaze toward the city below.

"I can't help it," Liora said with a smirk. "A lot's happened."

Kael nodded, his expression thoughtful. "Yeah. It has."

They stood in comfortable silence for a moment, the breeze gently tugging at their clothes. Liora's heart felt lighter here, in the quiet of the evening, with Kael beside her. For the first time in what felt like forever, there was no curse hanging over them, no immediate danger, no looming threat.

Just peace.

"You never told me," Kael said quietly, breaking the silence. "Why did you really agree to help me? Was it just because of the deal?"

Liora hesitated, her heart skipping a beat. She had asked herself that question so many times, especially in the beginning. At first, it had been about survival—a way to avoid punishment, a way to escape her past. But now... it was something more.

"No," Liora said softly, her voice steady. "It wasn't just about the deal."

Kael's eyes flicked to hers, a faint smile tugging at his lips. "Then why?"

Liora's chest tightened as she met his gaze, the weight of her feelings pressing down on her. She could see the raw vulnerability in his eyes, the quiet fear that he still wasn't enough, that he didn't deserve the happiness he had found.

But he did.

"Because I care about you," Liora said, her voice barely above a whisper. "Because you're worth it."

Kael's breath hitched, his eyes softening with emotion. For a moment, they stood there, the distance between them closing, until finally, Kael reached out, his fingers brushing her cheek.

"And I care about you," Kael whispered, his voice filled with quiet intensity.

Liora's heart raced as she leaned into his touch, her eyes searching his. There was something fragile and beautiful in this moment, something that made her chest ache with emotion.

And then, with a soft, tentative movement, Kael leaned in and kissed her.

The world seemed to fall away. The quiet of the evening, the city below, the palace around them—it all faded into the background as Liora lost herself in the warmth of his kiss, the gentle press of his lips against hers. It wasn't desperate or frantic—it was slow, filled with all the emotions they had been holding back for so long.

When they finally pulled apart, Kael's eyes were filled with something soft, something real.

"Liora," he whispered, his voice trembling with emotion. "Thank you."

Liora smiled, her chest full to bursting with everything she felt for him. "You don't have to thank me."

Kael smiled softly, his hand still resting against her cheek. "I know. But I want to."

They stood together, the sun setting behind them, casting the world in shades of gold and amber. And in that moment, Liora knew that no matter what challenges lay ahead, no matter what the future held, they would face it together.

The days that followed Kael's return were filled with the bustle of the kingdom preparing for a new era. The court was abuzz with plans for Kael's coronation, dignitaries from across the realm arrived to offer their congratulations, and the people of Solstraea celebrated the end of the prince's long slumber.

But amid the excitement, Liora and Kael found quiet moments to themselves—moments where they could simply be together, away from the eyes of the court, away from the expectations of the crown.

It was in those quiet moments that Liora began to imagine a new future—one she had never thought possible.

They were sitting in the palace gardens one afternoon, the soft hum of bees and the scent of roses filling the air. Liora leaned back against a stone bench, her fingers absentmindedly playing with a small, delicate rose petal she had plucked from a nearby bush.

Kael sat beside her, his head tilted back as he basked in

the warmth of the sun. He looked peaceful here, in the garden, away from the pressures of the throne. It reminded Liora of the Kael she had first met in the Dreamplane— the boy trapped in a world of crumbling memories, fighting against a curse he hadn't deserved.

"How does it feel?" Liora asked, her voice breaking the comfortable silence.

Kael opened one eye, glancing at her with a lazy smile. "How does what feel?"

"Being free," Liora said, her tone soft but serious.

Kael's smile faded slightly, and he was quiet for a moment, his gaze distant. "It feels... strange. Good, but strange. Like I've been given a second chance, and I'm still trying to figure out what to do with it."

Liora nodded, her heart tightening at the vulnerability in his voice. "You'll figure it out."

Kael's eyes flicked to hers, his expression thoughtful. "I know. And I want you to be a part of that."

Liora's breath caught in her throat. "What do you mean?"

Kael shifted, turning to face her fully, his gaze serious. "You don't have to stay, you know. You're not bound to the palace or to me. If you want to leave, to go back to your old life—"

"I don't want that," Liora interrupted, her voice firm. "My old life... it's not who I am anymore. And I don't want to be anywhere but here."

Kael's eyes softened, his expression filled with quiet relief. "Are you sure? I don't want you to feel trapped."

Liora smiled, her heart full. "I'm not trapped, Kael. I'm exactly where I want to be."

Kael's gaze held hers, filled with gratitude and something deeper—something that made Liora's chest tighten with emotion.

"I don't know what the future holds," Kael said quietly, his voice steady. "But I want to face it with you. I can't imagine doing this without you."

Liora's heart swelled with emotion, and for a moment, she couldn't find the words. But she didn't need them. She reached out, her hand slipping into his, and Kael's fingers tightened around hers.

"You're stuck with me now," Liora said with a smirk, her tone light but filled with meaning.

Kael laughed softly, his eyes twinkling with warmth. "Good. Because I wouldn't have it any other way."

They sat together in the garden, hand in hand, the future stretching out before them like an open road. And for the first time in a long time, Liora felt a deep, unshakable sense of hope—a belief that no matter what challenges lay ahead, they would face them together.

The night of Kael's coronation arrived sooner than either of them expected. The palace was alive with activity—courtiers and dignitaries filled the grand hall, the air buzzing with anticipation. The people of Solstraea had gathered outside the palace walls, eager to see their new king crowned.

But for Kael and Liora, the most important moment wasn't the ceremony or the speeches. It was the quiet moment just before, when they stood together on the palace balcony, looking out over the kingdom they had fought so hard to protect.

Kael stood in his formal royal attire, the weight of the crown soon to be placed on his head pressing down on him. But when he looked at Liora, standing beside him in her simple but elegant dress, the tension seemed to melt away.

"You ready?" Liora asked, her voice soft but teasing.

Kael smiled, his eyes warm. "As ready as I'll ever be."

Liora smirked. "You'll do great."

Kael's smile widened, and for a moment, they stood in comfortable silence, the world below them alive with celebration.

Then, Kael turned to her, his expression serious. "Liora, before all of this happens... I need you to know something."

Liora raised an eyebrow, her heart skipping a beat. "What?"

Kael's hand slipped into hers, his fingers tightening around hers with quiet certainty. "No matter what happens, no matter what the future holds—I want you by my side. Always."

Liora's breath hitched, her chest tightening with emotion. She could see the raw sincerity in his eyes, the quiet promise behind his words.

"I want that, too," Liora whispered, her voice filled with quiet determination.

Kael's lips twitched into a soft smile, and for a moment, the weight of everything seemed to disappear. The future, the crown, the kingdom—it all faded away, leaving only the two of them, standing together in the quiet of the night.

And in that moment, Liora knew that no matter what challenges lay ahead, no matter how difficult the road might be, they would face it together.

Hand in hand.

Always.

CHAPTER 8
A KINGDOM REBORN

The throne room was packed with nobles, advisors, and dignitaries from across the realm, all gathered to witness the formal coronation of Prince Kael. The air was thick with the scent of incense and the low murmur of voices, but a heavy silence fell over the crowd as Kael took his first steps toward the throne.

Liora watched from the side, standing among the courtiers, her heart pounding in her chest. She had never seen Kael like this before—dressed in the royal robes, his face set in a mask of calm confidence. He looked every bit the king he was meant to be, but Liora could sense the tension in him. She knew him well enough to recognize the tightness in his shoulders, the slight hesitation in his step.

The crown, gleaming gold and studded with jewels, was held by Callia, who stood at the head of the room, waiting to place it on Kael's head. As Kael approached the throne, he paused for a moment, his gaze flicking to Liora.

Their eyes met, and for a brief second, the weight of

the moment seemed to ease. Liora gave him a small, reassuring smile, and Kael's lips twitched, a hint of his real self breaking through the royal mask.

Then, with a deep breath, he stepped forward and knelt before the throne.

Callia's voice rang out, clear and strong. "By the power vested in me by the crown of Solstraea, I declare Kael, son of King Aeron, the rightful king of this realm."

The crown was lowered onto Kael's head, and as the heavy weight of it settled in place, Liora could see the shift in him. The boy who had once been trapped in the Dreamplane, haunted by his father's curse, was now the ruler of an entire kingdom.

A king.

The nobles erupted into applause, and the sound of it echoed through the vast hall, filling the air with a sense of celebration and renewal. Liora's heart swelled with pride as she watched Kael rise to his feet, his expression calm and composed.

He was a king now, but to her, he was still Kael—the boy who had fought beside her, the boy who had opened his heart to her in the quiet moments between battles.

And as Kael turned to face the crowd, his gaze once again finding hers, Liora knew that no matter what challenges lay ahead, they would face them together.

Life in the palace was nothing like the life Liora had known before.

She had spent most of her life on the streets, a thief

and an outcast, always looking over her shoulder, always ready to run. But here, in the grand halls of Solstraea's palace, everything was different. The walls were lined with tapestries and paintings, the floors polished marble, and everywhere she turned, there were guards and servants moving about with quiet efficiency.

It was overwhelming, to say the least.

Liora had never been one for luxury, and the thought of living in a place like this, surrounded by wealth and power, made her feel out of place. But Kael had insisted that she stay—that she was part of this new life he was building.

"You're not just a guest," Kael had told her one night as they sat together in the garden. "You're part of this. You're part of me."

Those words had warmed her heart, but they hadn't erased the doubts that still lingered at the edges of her mind. How could she, a girl from the streets, ever fit into a world like this?

The palace staff had been polite to her, but she could feel their curious stares, the quiet murmurs behind her back. Liora had quickly earned a reputation as the prince's mysterious companion, the girl who had helped him break the curse, but she still felt like an outsider.

One afternoon, as she wandered through the palace gardens, Liora found herself thinking back to her old life —before Kael, before the Dreamplane, before the curse. It seemed so distant now, like a different lifetime. But the memories were still there, lurking in the corners of her mind, reminding her of who she had been.

A thief. A nobody.

Liora's fingers brushed the delicate petals of a rose, the familiar hum of her magic stirring beneath her skin. The thorns that had once been her weapon, her shield, now felt different. They were still part of her, but they no longer defined her.

She had changed. And maybe that was what scared her the most.

"You look like you're a thousand miles away," a voice said, breaking through her thoughts.

Liora turned to see Kael standing at the edge of the garden, a soft smile on his lips. He was dressed in his formal robes, the crown no longer on his head but still heavy on his shoulders.

"Just thinking," Liora said, forcing a smile. "Palace life is... different."

Kael's smile faded slightly as he stepped closer, his eyes searching hers. "You're not happy here, are you?"

Liora hesitated, her heart tightening. "It's not that. It's just... I'm not used to this. All of this."

Kael's gaze softened, and he reached out, his hand brushing hers. "You don't have to be anyone but yourself, Liora. I don't care about the palace or the titles. I care about you."

Liora's breath hitched, her chest tightening with emotion. She had always been so used to hiding her feelings, to keeping people at a distance. But with Kael, it was different. He saw her—the real her—and that terrified her as much as it comforted her.

"I know," Liora whispered, her voice trembling slightly. "But sometimes I wonder... if I'm enough for this."

Kael's hand tightened around hers, his voice firm. "You are enough. More than enough."

Liora looked up at him, her heart swelling with gratitude and something deeper—something that made her feel like she belonged, not just in the palace, but with him.

Kael smiled softly, his eyes warm. "You're not alone, Liora. We'll figure this out together."

And in that moment, standing in the quiet of the garden, Liora realized that no matter how different her life had become, she wasn't the same girl who had once stolen to survive. She had found something more—something worth fighting for.

And she wasn't going to let it slip away.

That evening, the palace was alive with music and laughter as the coronation ball got underway. The grand ballroom was filled with noblemen and women, all dressed in their finest attire, their faces glowing with excitement and celebration.

Liora stood at the edge of the ballroom, watching as the guests danced and mingled, their laughter echoing through the vast hall. She had never seen anything like it —so much wealth, so much beauty. It felt like a world apart from the life she had known.

But despite the grandeur of the event, Liora couldn't shake the feeling of unease that had settled in her chest. The attention—the stares—were almost suffocating. She could feel the eyes of the nobles on her, watching her, judging her and finding her lacking.

She didn't belong here. Not really.

But then, she saw Kael.

He was standing near the center of the room, surrounded by dignitaries and courtiers, but his gaze was fixed on her. The moment their eyes met, a smile broke across his face, and Liora's heart skipped a beat.

Kael excused himself from the conversation and made his way toward her, his steps confident and sure. He looked every bit the king he had become—strong, poised, and ready to lead. But to Liora, he was still the boy she had met in the Dreamplane, the boy who had stolen her heart.

"You look beautiful," Kael said as he reached her, his voice soft.

Liora blushed, glancing down at the simple dress she had chosen for the evening. It wasn't nearly as elaborate as the gowns worn by the noblewomen around her, but it was comfortable, and that was all that mattered to her.

"Thanks," Liora said with a smirk. "You don't look so bad yourself."

Kael chuckled, his eyes twinkling with amusement. "Care to dance?"

Liora's heart skipped a beat. "I'm not exactly the dancing type."

Kael's smile widened, and he held out his hand. "Lucky for you, I am."

Liora hesitated for a moment, her mind racing with doubts. But then, she saw the warmth in Kael's eyes, the quiet reassurance that she didn't have to be anyone but herself.

And so, she took his hand.

Kael led her onto the dance floor, and as the music

swelled around them, Liora found herself relaxing in his arms. They moved together, slowly at first, but as the rhythm of the music swept them up, Liora felt herself letting go of her doubts, her fears.

For the first time in a long time, she wasn't worried about what people thought of her, or whether she belonged. All that mattered was this moment—dancing with Kael, feeling the warmth of his hand in hers, the steady beat of his heart against her own.

They danced through the night, the world around them fading into the background, until it was just the two of them, lost in the music, in each other.

As the night drew on and the guests began to retire, Liora and Kael found a quiet moment together on the palace balcony, looking out over the city of Solstraea. The stars glittered above them, and the soft breeze carried the distant sounds of celebration from the streets below.

Kael leaned against the railing, his expression relaxed for the first time in hours. "I never thought I'd be standing here as king," he said quietly.

Liora smiled, stepping closer to him. "And how does it feel?"

Kael glanced at her, his eyes thoughtful. "It feels... right. But also terrifying."

Liora chuckled. "That sounds about right."

Kael's smile faded slightly, and he turned to face her fully. "And you? Are you alright with all of this? The palace, the crown... everything?"

Liora hesitated, her heart tightening. She had been asking herself that same question for days, wondering if she could truly fit into this new life. But now, standing here with Kael, she knew the answer.

"I am," Liora said softly, her voice steady. "As long as I'm with you, I'm alright."

Kael's eyes softened, and for a moment, they stood in comfortable silence, the weight of the evening settling around them.

But then, a figure stepped out from the shadows.

Liora's breath caught in her throat as she turned, her heart racing. A man stood at the edge of the balcony, dressed in dark, simple clothing, his face hidden by the hood of his cloak. He moved with quiet, deliberate steps, his presence almost ghostly in the soft moonlight.

Kael's body tensed, his hand moving instinctively to Liora's arm, pulling her behind him. "Who are you?" Kael demanded, his voice sharp.

The man didn't answer immediately. Instead, he stepped forward, his hood falling back to reveal a face lined with age and wisdom. His eyes were sharp, glinting in the moonlight, and his lips curled into a faint smile.

"You've done well, Your Highness," the man said, his voice low and smooth. "But your journey is far from over."

Kael frowned, his hand tightening around Liora's. "What do you mean?"

The man's smile widened. "There are forces at work far beyond the curse you've broken. Darker forces. And they are watching you."

Liora's pulse quickened, her mind racing. **Darker forces?** After everything they had been through, the thought of another threat looming on the horizon sent a chill down her spine.

Kael's expression hardened. "What do you know?"

The man chuckled softly. "All in good time, Your Highness. But for now, be wary. The shadows are stirring, and your kingdom is not as safe as you think."

With that, the man turned and disappeared into the darkness, leaving Kael and Liora standing in stunned silence on the balcony.

Liora's heart pounded in her chest as she turned to Kael, her mind racing with questions. "Who was that?"

Kael's eyes were dark, his expression tense. "I don't know. But we need to find out."

The next morning, Liora and Kael were on edge. The encounter with the mysterious stranger had left them both unsettled, and the cryptic warning about darker forces stirred an unease they couldn't shake.

As the first light of dawn filtered through the palace windows, Kael stood at the edge of the balcony, staring out over the city with a frown. His hand rested on the hilt of the sword at his side, a clear sign that he was ready for whatever might come.

Liora joined him, her heart heavy with worry. "Do you think he was telling the truth?"

Kael's brow furrowed, his gaze distant. "I don't know. But we can't ignore the possibility."

Liora nodded, her mind spinning with thoughts of the stranger's warning. **Darker forces.** The words echoed in her mind, filling her with a sense of foreboding.

"We've faced darkness before," Liora said quietly, her voice steady. "And we beat it. We'll do it again."

Kael's eyes softened as he turned to her, his expression filled with a quiet determination. "You're right. We will."

For a moment, they stood in silence, the weight of the future pressing down on them. But this time, it wasn't just the threat of the curse or the burden of the crown that weighed on them—it was the knowledge that their journey was far from over.

There were still battles to be fought, still shadows to face.

But they would face them together.

Kael reached out, his hand slipping into hers, and Liora's heart swelled with a mix of fear and hope. The road ahead might be filled with challenges, but they had come too far to turn back now.

"We'll figure this out," Kael said quietly, his voice filled with resolve.

Liora nodded, her chest tight with emotion. "Always."

As the sun rose higher in the sky, casting its light over the kingdom of Solstraea, Liora knew that they were standing on the edge of something new—something bigger than either of them could have imagined.

But for the first time, she wasn't afraid.

Because no matter what challenges lay ahead, no matter how dark the shadows might grow, they would face them together.

And that was all that mattered.

CHAPTER 9

THE GATHERING STORM

The air in Solstraea was heavy with unease. It had been days since the mysterious visitor appeared on the palace balcony, his cryptic warning lingering like a shadow over everything. Scouts were returning with troubling reports from the outer regions of the kingdom—strange movements in the forests, sightings of cloaked figures, whispers of dark magic in places that had long been abandoned.

The kingdom was not as safe as it seemed.

Kael stood in the war room, his eyes scanning the map of Solstraea spread out before him. His fingers traced the borderlands where most of the activity had been reported, his brow furrowed in concentration. Liora stood at his side, silent but watchful. She could feel the tension radiating from him, the weight of leadership pressing down on his shoulders.

"We need to act," Kael said, his voice low but firm. "We can't wait for this threat to come to us."

Liora nodded, her mind racing. The unease she had felt

since the stranger's visit had only grown stronger. There was something out there, something dangerous, and it was coming for them. She could feel it, like a storm brewing on the horizon.

"We need more information," she said, her voice steady. "The scouts have seen things, but we still don't know what we're up against."

Kael's gaze flicked to hers, a shadow of doubt in his eyes. "We could be walking into something we're not prepared for."

Liora stepped closer, her hand resting lightly on his arm. "We've faced the unknown before. We can handle this."

Kael's jaw tightened, but he nodded, his resolve hardening. "Then we'll send more scouts. I want to know exactly what we're dealing with."

As they turned to leave the war room, Callia entered, her expression grim. "Your Highness, there's been another report."

Kael's face darkened. "What is it?"

Callia hesitated for a moment, her eyes flicking to Liora before she spoke. "The scouts we sent to the northern borders... they've gone missing."

Liora's breath caught in her throat, her pulse quickening. **Missing?** She exchanged a glance with Kael, the unease in the room thickening like a shroud.

"What do you mean, 'missing'?" Kael asked, his voice tight.

Callia's expression was grave. "We've lost contact with them. They were last seen entering the Blackwood Forest. Since then, nothing."

The Blackwood Forest. Liora's stomach twisted. She had heard the stories about that place—stories of dark magic, of ancient curses that still lingered in the shadows. It was the kind of place people avoided, a place where even the bravest didn't dare to tread.

Kael's hands clenched into fists at his sides. "We need to find them."

Callia nodded. "I'm already preparing a search party. But... there's something else. The villagers near Blackwood have reported strange happenings—lights in the sky, unnatural sounds in the night. Whatever is out there, it's not just rumors anymore."

The weight of her words hung heavy in the air, and for a moment, no one spoke. Liora could feel the tension tightening around her, the sense that they were standing on the edge of something dangerous, something far bigger than any of them had anticipated.

"We need answers," Kael said quietly, his voice filled with quiet determination. "And we can't wait for the danger to come to us."

Liora stepped forward, her voice firm. "Then we go to Blackwood."

Kael turned to her, his eyes filled with concern. "Liora, it's too dangerous. We don't know what we're dealing with."

Liora's chest tightened, but she held his gaze. "I'm not letting you face this alone. Whatever's out there, we'll face it together."

Kael's expression softened, his eyes filled with gratitude and something deeper—something that made Liora's heart ache. "Together," he whispered, his voice filled with quiet resolve.

And in that moment, they both knew that whatever was coming—whatever darkness lay ahead—they would face it side by side.

The journey to the Blackwood Forest was tense, the air thick with the promise of danger. Kael had insisted on bringing a small contingent of his most trusted guards, but even they seemed uneasy as they approached the edge of the dark, sprawling woods.

The forest loomed ahead of them, its twisted trees rising like black spires against the gray sky. The air was colder here, the wind carrying a faint, unsettling whisper that made the hairs on the back of Liora's neck stand on end.

As they dismounted their horses and approached the forest's entrance, Liora felt the weight of the place pressing down on her. The stories about Blackwood weren't just tales to scare children. There was something unnatural here, something old and malevolent that seemed to watch them from the shadows.

Kael walked beside her, his face set in a grim expression. "Stay close," he said, his voice low.

Liora nodded, her hand resting on the hilt of her dagger. The thorns pulsed beneath her skin, her magic humming with the tension in the air. She could feel the forest, the way it seemed to breathe, to shift around them, as if it were alive.

They moved deeper into the woods, the trees closing in around them like a living wall. The light grew dimmer, the shadows longer, and Liora's pulse quickened as the sense of danger grew stronger with every step.

"What is this place?" one of the guards muttered, his voice trembling slightly.

"Blackwood has always been cursed," Callia said quietly, her eyes scanning the treetops. "But there's something new here. Something darker."

As they continued deeper into the forest, a low, rumbling sound echoed through the trees—a sound that sent a chill down Liora's spine. The guards exchanged uneasy glances, their hands tightening on their weapons.

Liora's heart raced, her instincts screaming that something was wrong. "We need to be careful," she whispered, her voice barely audible.

Kael's gaze flicked to hers, his jaw tight. "We're not turning back."

They pressed on, the sound growing louder, more ominous. And then, without warning, the trees parted, revealing a clearing at the center of the forest.

Liora's breath caught in her throat.

At the center of the clearing stood a massive stone structure, half-buried in the earth. It looked ancient, weathered by time and magic, its surface covered in strange, glowing runes that pulsed with a faint, eerie light.

"This is it," Callia said quietly, her voice filled with awe. "This is what the scouts were looking for."

Kael stepped forward, his eyes narrowing as he studied the stone. "What is it?"

Callia shook her head, her expression grave. "I don't know. But whatever it is, it's not natural."

Liora's pulse quickened as she approached the stone, her fingers brushing the strange runes. The moment her skin touched the surface, a sharp jolt of magic shot through her, making her gasp.

"Liora?" Kael's voice was filled with concern, and he reached for her arm. "What is it?"

Liora shook her head, her mind reeling. "This magic... it's old. Older than anything I've ever felt."

The air around them seemed to hum with energy, the wind picking up, carrying with it a low, whispering sound that sent shivers down Liora's spine.

"We need to leave," one of the guards said, his voice trembling. "This place isn't right."

But before anyone could respond, the ground beneath their feet began to tremble.

Liora's heart raced as the runes on the stone flared with a sudden, blinding light. The air crackled with energy, and the whispering sound grew louder, more insistent, like a thousand voices speaking at once.

And then, from the shadows at the edge of the clearing, figures began to emerge.

Cloaked in darkness, their faces hidden by hoods, the figures moved with a slow, deliberate grace, their eyes glowing faintly in the dim light. Liora's breath caught in her throat as she counted them—six, seven, eight—each one moving silently toward them, their movements unnatural, like shadows come to life.

Kael's hand tightened around the hilt of his sword, his voice low and steady. "Everyone, stay alert."

Liora's magic surged under her skin, the thorns pulsing with energy as she prepared for whatever was coming. She could feel the danger radiating from the figures, the dark magic that clung to them like a shroud.

And then, one of the figures stepped forward, its voice a low, eerie whisper that seemed to echo in the air around them.

"You should not have come here, King of Solstraea."

Kael's jaw tightened, his sword drawn. "Who are you?"

The figure's hood tilted slightly, as if considering the question. "We are the ones who have watched from the shadows. The ones who have waited for the time to come."

Liora's pulse quickened, her heart racing. **The stranger's warning.** This was what he had been talking about. This was the darkness that had been stirring in the corners of their world, waiting for the right moment to strike.

"What do you want?" Kael demanded, his voice filled with authority.

The figure's glowing eyes flicked to Kael, and for a moment, the air seemed to freeze.

"We want what was promised to us," the figure said quietly, its voice like the rustling of dead leaves. "And we will take it. By any means necessary."

The figures moved closer, their cloaks rustling in the wind, their eyes glowing with dark intent. Liora's heart pounded in her chest as she stepped forward, her magic humming with energy. She didn't know who these people were, or what they wanted, but she wasn't going to let them hurt Kael.

"Stay back," Liora warned, her voice steady but filled with tension.

The lead figure's gaze shifted to her, and for a moment, it seemed to study her, its glowing eyes narrowing. "Ah, the girl with the thorns. You are not as invisible as you think."

Liora's blood ran cold.

The figure's voice dropped to a low whisper. "You should leave this place, child. Before it consumes you."

Kael stepped forward, his sword raised. "She's not going anywhere."

The figure's lips curled into a slow, sinister smile. "Then you have already sealed your fate, King of Solstraea."

Before anyone could react, the air around them exploded with dark magic. The ground shook, the wind howling as the figures lunged toward them, their movements swift and deadly.

Kael moved quickly, his sword flashing as he blocked the first attack, his body tense with focus. Liora's magic surged to life, the thorns snapping to attention as she threw herself into the fight. The guards were quick to follow, their swords clashing against the dark figures, but the battle was far from easy.

These figures weren't human—not entirely. Their movements were too fast, too fluid, their bodies shifting like shadows as they dodged attacks with terrifying ease. Liora's heart raced as she fought, her magic straining under the weight of the dark energy that filled the air.

"We're outnumbered," one of the guards shouted, his voice filled with panic.

"We can't hold them off forever," Callia said, her voice tense as she cast a spell, sending a blast of light toward one of the figures.

Kael gritted his teeth, his sword slicing through the air as he fought off another attacker. "We don't have to hold them off. We just need to get out of here."

Liora's pulse quickened as she realized the truth of his words. They were outmatched. Whatever these figures were, they weren't going to win this fight. Not here. Not now.

"We need to retreat," Liora shouted, her voice barely audible over the sound of the battle.

Kael hesitated for a moment, his eyes scanning the battlefield. But then, with a grim nod, he called out to the guards. "Fall back!"

The retreat was chaotic, the guards scrambling to fend off the dark figures as they made their way back toward the edge of the forest. Liora fought beside Kael, her magic pulsing with every strike, but she could feel her strength waning, the darkness pressing in on all sides.

As they reached the edge of the clearing, the lead figure's voice echoed through the trees, a low, ominous warning.

"You cannot escape what is coming, King of Solstraea. The shadows will find you, no matter where you hide."

Liora's heart pounded as they made their way out of the forest, the words of the dark figure ringing in her ears.

The shadows will find you.

By the time they returned to the palace, the tension was palpable. The battle in the Blackwood Forest had shaken them all, and the reality of the threat they faced had become painfully clear.

Kael paced in the war room, his expression grim, his hand clenched tightly around the hilt of his sword. Liora stood by the window, her thoughts racing. She had never felt anything like the magic in Blackwood—it was ancient, dangerous, and it was coming for them.

"We can't ignore this anymore," Kael said, his voice low but steady. "Whatever those figures were, they're not going to stop."

Callia, who had been studying the map of the kingdom, nodded. "They're organized. And powerful. If we don't act, they'll strike again. And next time, we might not be so lucky."

Liora turned to Kael, her heart heavy with the weight of the decision they faced. "What do we do?"

Kael's eyes flicked to hers, and for a moment, the vulnerability in his expression made her chest tighten. He was still new to this—new to being king, new to leading his people through a crisis. But despite his doubts, there was a quiet strength in him, a resolve that had been forged in the fires of everything they had faced together.

"We fight," Kael said quietly, his voice filled with determination. "We protect the kingdom. We protect each other."

Liora nodded, her pulse quickening. She had been by

Kael's side through every battle, every challenge, and she wasn't about to abandon him now.

But even as they made their plans, even as they prepared for the fight ahead, Liora couldn't shake the feeling that this was just the beginning—that the darkness they had glimpsed in Blackwood was only a small piece of something much larger, something that threatened not just Solstraea, but everything they had fought for.

The shadows were rising.

And they weren't ready.

That night, as the palace settled into a tense, uneasy silence, Liora found herself standing on the balcony, staring out over the city of Solstraea. The lights of the city flickered in the distance, but the air felt heavy, as though the darkness from Blackwood had followed them back to the palace.

Kael joined her a moment later, his footsteps quiet as he approached. He stood beside her, his expression thoughtful, but Liora could see the worry in his eyes.

Kael stood in silence, his eyes fixed on the horizon, but the tension in his posture spoke louder than any words. His hand rested on the stone railing, fingers clenched so tight that his knuckles were white.

"The soldiers are prepared," Liora said, more a question than a statement, watching his hand, waiting for him to respond.

A beat passed before Kael finally exhaled, shaking his

head slightly. "Prepared?" His voice was soft, distant. "Is anyone ever really prepared for what's coming?"

Liora swallowed the lump in her throat, her fingers brushing against his hand. "We've faced worse."

"Have we?" His smile was faint, brittle, as if he were trying to convince himself. His eyes never left the horizon.

Liora turned to him, her chest tight with emotion. "I am."

For a long moment, they stood in silence, the weight of the future pressing down on them. But even as the shadows gathered on the horizon, even as the threat of the unknown loomed larger than ever, Liora knew that they would face it together.

And no matter what came next, no matter how dark the path ahead might be, they wouldn't face it alone.

The storm was coming.

But they were ready to fight.

CHAPTER 10

INTO THE SHADOWS

The sky over Solstraea was gray and foreboding, the sun barely visible behind thick clouds that seemed to mirror the growing tension in the kingdom. Word of the strange happenings in the Blackwood Forest had begun to spread, and although Kael had kept the full truth from the public, rumors were swirling like wildfire.

Liora could feel the change in the air as she walked through the palace halls, the weight of impending conflict pressing down on everyone. The guards were on high alert, their eyes sharp, their movements tense. Courtiers whispered in hushed voices as they passed, their expressions filled with worry. Even the palace staff seemed uneasy, their footsteps quick and quiet, as if they could sense that something dark was approaching.

Liora's thoughts were filled with the memory of the battle in Blackwood. The strange figures, the dark magic, the warning that had echoed in her mind since they had escaped the forest: **The shadows will find you.**

And they were running out of time to stop them.

When she reached the war room, Kael was already there, standing over the large map of Solstraea that had become the center of their strategy. His face was drawn, his eyes filled with a quiet determination, but Liora could see the exhaustion creeping in around the edges. He hadn't slept much since they had returned from Blackwood, and the weight of leading a kingdom on the brink of disaster was beginning to show.

"Any news?" Liora asked, stepping up beside him.

Kael's gaze flicked to hers, but the smile didn't reach his eyes. "Callia's working on it. But the forest isn't in a hurry to give up its secrets."

Liora crossed her arms, feeling the weight of urgency tightening in her chest. "Secrets won't stop them from gaining power."

Kael's nod was slow, but his eyes remained fixed on the map, as if the lines could offer him answers. "Running in with half the picture could lose us everything."

Liora's chest tightened as she looked at the map. The forest was a dark blot on the otherwise peaceful landscape, a place of ancient magic and forgotten secrets. She had felt it the moment they had entered—that cold, oppressive force that seemed to seep into her bones. Whatever was hiding there, it was powerful, and it wasn't going to stop until it had what it wanted.

"What do you think they meant by 'what was promised to them'?" Liora asked quietly, her mind still turning over the cryptic words of the dark figures.

Kael's jaw tightened, and he let out a long, weary sigh. "I don't know. But whatever it is, they're willing to destroy the kingdom to get it."

Liora's heart ached at the weight in his voice. Kael had spent his whole life trapped by the curse, fighting against the shadow of his father's legacy. Now, just when he had begun to step into his role as king, another darkness had risen to challenge him. It wasn't fair—but then, nothing about their journey had ever been fair.

"We'll figure it out," Liora said, her voice filled with quiet determination. "We always do."

Kael's gaze softened, and for a moment, the tension in his body seemed to ease. "I couldn't do this without you."

Liora's breath hitched, her heart tightening with emotion. "You're not alone, Kael. We're in this together."

Kael smiled, but before he could respond, the doors to the war room opened, and Callia entered, her expression tense.

"Your Highness," she said, her voice clipped. "We've received a message from the northern border."

Kael's face darkened. "What is it?"

Callia handed him a small, rolled parchment, her eyes filled with worry. "It's from one of our scouts. They've spotted movement—large groups of people, moving toward the forest."

Liora's pulse quickened, her mind racing. **More of them.**

Kael unrolled the parchment, his eyes scanning the message quickly. His expression grew darker with every word. "They're massing," he said quietly. "Preparing for something."

Liora's chest tightened. "An attack."

Callia nodded grimly. "That's what it looks like.

They're gathering forces, likely waiting for the right moment to strike."

Kael set the parchment down, his jaw clenched. "Then we need to be ready."

The weight of his words hung heavy in the air, and for a moment, the three of them stood in silence, the reality of the situation settling over them like a dark cloud.

"We'll need to rally the troops," Callia said, her voice steady despite the tension. "Prepare the city's defenses. If they're planning an attack, it could come soon."

Kael nodded, his expression hardening with resolve. "Do it. We'll protect Solstraea at all costs."

Liora's heart raced as she looked at Kael. She could see the weight of leadership pressing down on him, the responsibility of protecting an entire kingdom resting on his shoulders. But she also saw his strength—his quiet determination to do whatever it took to keep his people safe.

And she would be right beside him through it all.

The days that followed were filled with a flurry of preparations. The palace became a hive of activity, with soldiers moving in and out of the city, gathering supplies, and fortifying defenses. The people of Solstraea, sensing the growing danger, had become more anxious, their eyes filled with fear as they whispered about the shadowy figures that had been seen in the north.

Liora spent most of her time at Kael's side, helping him coordinate the preparations. She had never been a soldier, but her instincts from years of survival on the streets proved useful in planning for the unexpected. Kael listened to her advice, valuing her input as much as that of his advisors.

But even as they prepared for the coming battle, there was a quiet tension between them—an unspoken fear that neither of them wanted to acknowledge.

"What if we're not ready?" Liora asked one night, as they stood together on the balcony, looking out over the city. The moon hung low in the sky, casting a pale light over the streets below.

Kael was silent for a moment, his gaze distant. "I've asked myself the same thing," he admitted quietly. "But I can't think that way. I have to believe that we'll be ready. That we'll win."

Liora's chest tightened as she looked at him. She could see the doubt flickering in his eyes, the quiet fear that he wasn't enough—that he would fail his people, his kingdom.

"You are ready," Liora said firmly, her voice filled with conviction. "You've already proven that. You broke the curse. You became king. You've faced every challenge that's come your way and survived. You'll survive this, too."

Kael's gaze softened, and he smiled faintly. "You make it sound easy."

Liora smirked, her heart lighter for a moment. "It's not. But you're not alone. You don't have to carry this weight by yourself."

Kael's hand slipped into hers, his touch warm and steady. "I know. And I'm grateful for that."

For a moment, they stood in comfortable silence, the weight of their connection grounding them in the face of the uncertainty ahead. But even in the quiet of the night, Liora could feel the storm brewing on the horizon—the dark forces gathering, waiting for the right moment to strike.

And she knew that when the time came, they would have to fight for everything they had built.

The morning air was crisp as Kael and Liora stood on the city walls, looking out over the vast plains that stretched toward the Blackwood Forest. The sun had barely risen, casting a pale golden light over the landscape, but the tension in the air was unmistakable.

In the distance, near the edge of the forest, Liora could see movement—dark figures shifting in and out of the shadows, their cloaks blending into the gloom. The sight of them sent a chill down her spine, a reminder of the battle that was fast approaching.

"They're getting bolder," Kael muttered, his eyes narrowed as he watched the figures move. "They're not even trying to hide anymore."

Liora's pulse quickened, her hand resting on the hilt of her dagger. "They want us to see them. They're trying to scare us."

Kael's jaw tightened. "It won't work."

Liora admired his determination, but she couldn't shake the feeling that the dark figures were more dangerous than they appeared. There was something unnatural about them, something that went beyond simple intimidation. They were planning something, and whatever it was, it wasn't going to be easy to stop.

As they continued to watch the distant figures, a soldier approached, his expression tense. "Your Highness, the scouts have returned."

Kael turned to the soldier, his face set in a grim expression. "What did they find?"

The soldier hesitated, his eyes flicking nervously between Kael and Liora. "They spotted movement near the forest, large groups of people gathering. But... they also found something else."

Liora's heart raced, her mind spinning. "What is it?"

The soldier's face paled as he spoke. "They found... bodies. Villagers from the northern settlements. But they weren't just killed. It looked like... dark magic."

Kael's expression hardened, and he nodded grimly. "Thank you. Dismissed."

As the soldier left, Liora felt a cold knot form in her stomach. **Dark magic.** It was what they had feared all along, the thing that had been hinted at in the cryptic warnings from Blackwood. The dark forces weren't just gathering—they were preparing to strike, and they were willing to use any means necessary to get what they wanted.

"We need to act," Liora said quietly, her voice filled with urgency.

Kael nodded, his eyes dark with resolve. "We will. But we need to be smart about it."

Liora's heart pounded in her chest as she looked out over the distant figures once more. The battle was coming, and it was going to be unlike anything they had faced before.

And they weren't ready.

By the time night fell, the war room was filled with Kael's closest advisors, Callia among them. The tension in the room was palpable, the air thick with the weight of the decisions that needed to be made.

"Their numbers are growing," Callia said, her voice calm but filled with urgency. "We can't wait much longer. If we don't act soon, they'll overwhelm us."

Kael stood at the head of the table, his expression grim but resolute. "We won't wait. We'll strike first."

Liora's pulse quickened as she listened, her mind racing. **Strike first?** It was a bold move, but she understood the necessity. Waiting would only give their enemies more time to gather strength, more time to prepare for an attack that could cripple the kingdom.

"We'll need to send a small force," Kael continued, his voice steady. "We can't risk an all-out assault without knowing exactly what we're up against. But we need to weaken their forces before they strike."

Callia nodded, her eyes sharp. "A strike team. In and out, before they have a chance to react."

Kael glanced at Liora, his expression filled with quiet determination. "I want you with me, Liora. We need your magic."

Liora's heart skipped a beat. She had known this moment was coming—the moment when she would have to face the dark forces head-on, using her magic to help protect the kingdom she had come to care for. But the thought of it still sent a thrill of fear through her.

"I'm with you," Liora said firmly, her voice steady despite the tension in her chest.

Kael's gaze softened, and for a moment, the weight of the battle ahead seemed to fade. "We'll do this together."

The plan was set, and the weight of it hung heavy over the room. The strike would happen at dawn, a small force slipping into the Blackwood to disrupt the enemy before they had a chance to launch their attack. It was a dangerous mission, but it was the only way to protect the kingdom from the growing threat.

As the meeting came to an end, Liora stood beside Kael, her heart pounding with a mix of fear and determination. She had been by his side through every battle, every challenge, and she wasn't going to stop now.

But as they prepared for the mission ahead, a nagging thought gnawed at the back of her mind—the warning from the dark figures: *The shadows will find you.*

She just hoped they were ready.

That night, as the palace settled into a tense silence, Liora found herself standing in her chamber, staring out at the darkened city below. The weight of the coming battle pressed down on her, her thoughts swirling with a mix of fear and determination.

A soft knock at the door broke through her musings,

and when she turned, Kael was standing in the doorway, his expression thoughtful.

"May I come in?" he asked quietly.

Liora nodded, her heart racing as he stepped into the room.

For a moment, they stood in silence, the tension of the day still hanging between them. But then, Kael crossed the room and reached for her hand, his touch warm and steady.

"Tomorrow's going to be hard," Kael said quietly, his voice filled with quiet resolve. "But I'm glad you're with me."

Liora's chest tightened, her heart swelling with emotion. "I wouldn't be anywhere else."

Kael smiled softly, but there was a flicker of worry in his eyes. "I just... I don't want anything to happen to you. I couldn't bear it."

Liora's breath hitched, her chest tightening with the weight of his words. She could feel the unspoken fears between them—the fear of losing each other, the fear that the battle ahead might be their last.

But she wasn't going to let fear control her.

"We'll be alright," Liora said firmly, her voice filled with quiet conviction. "We've survived worse."

Kael's gaze held hers, and for a moment, the weight of everything seemed to fade. He stepped closer, his hand cupping her cheek, his touch gentle but filled with emotion.

"I'm not ready to lose you," Kael whispered, his voice trembling.

Liora's heart ached, and she leaned into his touch, her eyes searching his. "You won't."

For a long moment, they stood together, the silence between them heavy with unspoken promises. And then, with a soft, tentative movement, Kael leaned in and kissed her.

It was slow, filled with all the emotions they had held back for so long—the fear, the hope, the love that had grown between them despite everything. Liora's heart raced as she kissed him back, her fingers tangling in his hair, her body melting into his.

When they finally pulled apart, Kael's eyes were filled with something raw, something real. "I love you," he whispered, his voice barely audible.

Liora's breath caught in her throat, her heart swelling with emotion. "I love you, too."

They stood together in the quiet of the night, their hands intertwined, the storm of the coming battle swirling around them. But in that moment, nothing else mattered.

They were together.

And they would face whatever came next—together.

CHAPTER II
INTO THE HEART OF DARKNESS

The sky was still dark when Kael, Liora, and the strike team gathered at the edge of Solstraea's city walls. The air was crisp, the wind biting at their skin as they prepared to set off for the Blackwood Forest. The only sound was the soft clinking of armor and weapons, the quiet murmur of the soldiers as they made final checks.

Liora stood beside Kael, her heart pounding in her chest. The weight of the mission pressed down on her, a knot of tension twisting in her stomach. This wasn't like any battle they had fought before. The dark figures lurking in the forest were unlike any enemy they had faced, and the magic that surrounded them was older, more dangerous than anything she had ever encountered.

"You ready?" Kael's voice was low, but steady.

Liora nodded, her hand resting on the hilt of her dagger. "As ready as I'll ever be."

Kael's gaze softened for a moment, his eyes filled with the same worry she had seen the night before. But there

123

was also something else—something that made her heart tighten. Determination. Hope. Love.

He reached out, his hand brushing hers for just a moment, a silent reassurance. "We'll get through this," he whispered. "Together."

Liora's breath caught in her throat, and she nodded, her chest tightening with emotion. "Together."

With that, Kael turned to the soldiers gathered around them, his expression hardening with resolve. "You all know the mission," he said, his voice steady. "We go in fast, disrupt their forces, and get out before they have a chance to regroup. Stay close, stay sharp, and don't take any unnecessary risks."

The soldiers nodded, their faces set in grim determination. Liora could see the tension in their bodies, the quiet fear that lingered in the air, but she knew that every one of them was ready to do whatever it took to protect Solstraea.

As the first light of dawn began to break over the horizon, they set off, their footsteps silent as they moved through the city gates and into the open plains beyond. The Blackwood Forest loomed in the distance, dark and foreboding, like a gaping wound in the landscape. Liora's pulse quickened as they drew closer, her magic humming under her skin, sensing the danger that lay ahead.

The strike team moved quickly, their movements precise and controlled, but as they neared the edge of the forest, the air grew colder, the wind carrying with it a faint, eerie whisper that sent a shiver down Liora's spine.

"They're close," Kael muttered, his hand tightening on the hilt of his sword.

Liora nodded, her senses on high alert. She could feel

the dark magic pulsing through the trees, the weight of it pressing down on her like a heavy fog. The shadows seemed to shift and move at the edges of her vision, and for a moment, she could have sworn she saw figures lurking in the darkness, watching them.

"We need to be careful," Liora whispered, her voice barely audible. "This place isn't right."

Kael's gaze flicked to hers, and he nodded grimly. "Stay close."

As they entered the forest, the trees closed in around them, the light fading to a dim, eerie glow that barely penetrated the thick canopy. The air was thick with the smell of damp earth and decay, and the sound of their footsteps was muffled by the soft, spongy ground beneath their feet.

Liora's heart raced as they moved deeper into the forest, her magic pulsing with energy, ready to react at the first sign of danger. She could feel the thorns stirring beneath her skin, a reminder of the power she carried, but also of the danger that came with it.

The strike team moved in silence, their eyes scanning the shadows for any sign of movement. The forest was eerily quiet, the only sound the faint rustle of leaves and the occasional creak of a tree branch.

But Liora knew better. The silence wasn't natural.

Something was watching them.

It happened without warning.

One moment, the forest was still, the strike team

moving cautiously through the trees. The next, the air was filled with a low, menacing whisper—like the rustling of dead leaves, but layered with a dark, insidious magic that made Liora's skin crawl.

"Get ready!" Kael shouted, drawing his sword in one fluid motion.

The strike team instantly shifted into a defensive formation, weapons drawn, eyes scanning the shadows. Liora's pulse quickened, her heart pounding in her chest as she reached for her dagger, her magic surging under her skin, the thorns snapping to life.

And then, from the darkness, they came.

Figures emerged from the shadows—cloaked in black, their faces hidden beneath hoods, their eyes glowing with the same eerie light that had haunted Liora since their first encounter. They moved with a terrifying grace, their bodies shifting like shadows as they closed in on the team.

Liora's breath hitched, her mind racing as she took in the sight of them. There were more than she had expected—far more. And they weren't just moving in for an attack. They were surrounding them, cutting off their escape.

"We're outnumbered," one of the soldiers muttered, his voice tense.

Kael's jaw tightened, his eyes narrowed. "We stick to the plan. Don't let them surround us."

The first of the dark figures lunged forward, moving with unnatural speed. Kael reacted instantly, his sword flashing in the dim light as he parried the attack, his body moving with the precision of a seasoned warrior. Liora followed suit, her magic flaring to life as she threw herself into the fight, her dagger cutting through the air with deadly accuracy.

The battle was chaotic, the sounds of metal clashing against metal, the shouts of soldiers, and the eerie whispers of the dark figures filling the air. Liora's heart raced as she fought, her body moving on instinct, her magic guiding her movements.

But even as they fought, Liora could feel the dark magic pressing in around them, suffocating them. The figures were stronger than she had expected, their movements too fast, too fluid. They weren't human—not entirely. They were something else, something born from the shadows.

"We're getting overwhelmed!" one of the soldiers shouted, his voice filled with panic.

Kael's sword sliced through the air as he fought off another attacker, his face set in a grim expression. "Hold the line!"

Liora's magic surged through her, the thorns snapping at the dark figures as they tried to close in on her. But for every one she cut down, two more seemed to take their place. Her chest tightened with fear as she realized that they were losing ground—fast.

"We need to fall back!" Liora shouted, her voice barely audible over the chaos.

Kael hesitated for a moment, his eyes scanning the battlefield. But he knew she was right. They couldn't win this fight—not like this.

"Retreat!" Kael shouted, his voice commanding. "Fall back to the clearing!"

The strike team moved as one, their movements coordinated as they began to retreat, cutting their way through the dark figures as they fought to reach the clearing. Liora stayed close to Kael, her magic flaring with every step, but the weight of the dark magic pressed down on her, making it harder to breathe, harder to focus.

As they reached the edge of the clearing, Kael turned, his sword raised as he blocked another attack. "Go! I'll hold them off!"

Liora's heart leapt into her throat. "No! We're not leaving you behind!"

Kael's gaze flicked to hers, filled with a mixture of determination and desperation. "I'll be right behind you! Go!"

Liora's chest tightened, her mind racing. She didn't want to leave him, didn't want to face the possibility of losing him. But she knew that if they didn't move now, they would all be lost.

With a sharp nod, Liora turned and followed the rest of the strike team into the clearing, her heart pounding in her chest as she fought to keep the fear at bay.

But as they reached the clearing, Liora felt the ground tremble beneath her feet.

And then, from the shadows, something far more dangerous emerged.

CHAPTER 12
THE DARK GUARDIAN

The air in the clearing seemed to thicken, the temperature dropping as the dark magic pulsed through the ground. Liora's breath caught in her throat as she turned to face the edge of the forest, her eyes widening at the sight of the figure emerging from the shadows.

It was massive—easily twice the size of the other dark figures, its body cloaked in a swirling mass of darkness. Its eyes glowed with an intense, malevolent light, and the air around it crackled with dark energy.

Liora's heart pounded in her chest, her body frozen with fear. This wasn't just one of the shadow figures. This was something else. Something far more dangerous.

The rest of the strike team hesitated, their weapons drawn, but none of them moved. The presence of the creature was overwhelming, its dark magic pressing down on them like a suffocating weight.

Kael arrived at her side, his sword raised, his face set in a grim expression. "What is that?"

Liora shook her head, her voice trembling. "I don't know. But it's powerful."

The dark figure stepped forward, its movements slow and deliberate, as if it had all the time in the world. The air around it shimmered with dark magic, the shadows twisting and writhing like living creatures.

"You should not have come here," the creature's voice echoed, deep and resonant, filling the air with a sense of dread. "This forest belongs to the shadows."

Liora's breath hitched, her heart racing as she felt the weight of the creature's words. There was something ancient about it—something that made her feel small and insignificant in the face of its power.

"We're not leaving," Kael said, his voice steady despite the fear that Liora could sense in him. "Whatever you're planning, it ends here."

The dark figure's lips curled into a slow, sinister smile. "Foolish king. You cannot stop what is already in motion."

Before anyone could react, the creature raised its hand, and a blast of dark energy shot toward them, crackling through the air like lightning.

Kael moved quickly, his sword flashing as he blocked the attack, but the force of it sent him stumbling back, his body trembling with the effort.

"Kael!" Liora shouted, rushing to his side, her magic flaring to life.

The dark figure stepped closer, its eyes glowing with malevolent intent. "This kingdom will fall. And you will fall with it."

Liora's heart pounded in her chest as she faced the creature, her magic pulsing beneath her skin. She could feel the thorns stirring, their power reacting to the dark magic that filled the air. But even as she prepared to fight, she knew that they were outmatched. This creature was too powerful—its magic too strong.

But they had no choice.

They had to fight.

The air crackled with dark energy as the creature raised its hand again, preparing to strike. Liora's magic flared in response, the thorns snapping to life around her as she threw herself in front of Kael, her dagger raised.

The blast of dark magic shot toward them, but Liora was ready. Her magic surged through her, the thorns wrapping around her in a protective barrier as she deflected the attack. The force of it sent a shockwave through her body, but she held firm, her feet planted in the soft earth.

Kael was at her side in an instant, his sword flashing as he parried another attack. "We need to weaken it!" he shouted over the roar of the magic.

Liora nodded, her mind racing as she tried to think of a way to do just that. The creature's dark magic was overwhelming, but there had to be a way to break through it. There had to be a weakness.

And then, in the chaos of the battle, she felt it.

The creature's magic—it was tied to the forest. To the shadows. It wasn't just using the darkness—it was drawing power from it. If they could disrupt that connection, they might have a chance.

"Kael!" Liora shouted, her voice filled with urgency. "It's tied to the forest! We need to cut off its power source!"

Kael's eyes flicked to her, his expression filled with determination. "How?"

Liora's heart raced as she scanned the clearing, her magic humming with energy. The thorns were still snapping at the dark figure, but they weren't strong enough to break through its defenses. They needed something more —something stronger.

And then, she saw it.

The stone structure—the same one they had found on their first journey into the forest. The ancient runes carved into its surface were glowing faintly, pulsing with a dark energy that mirrored the creature's power.

"That stone!" Liora shouted, pointing to the structure. "It's connected to the magic!"

Kael's gaze followed hers, and understanding dawned in his eyes. "If we destroy it..."

Liora nodded. "We weaken the creature."

With a sharp nod, Kael turned to the rest of the strike team. "Cover us! We need to destroy that stone!"

The soldiers moved quickly, their weapons raised as they formed a protective barrier around Kael and Liora, holding off the dark figures that continued to press in from the shadows.

Liora's magic flared to life as she and Kael rushed toward the stone, the thorns snapping at the dark energy that pulsed through the air. The runes glowed brighter as they approached, the power of them pressing down on her like a weight, but Liora didn't stop. She couldn't.

As they reached the stone, Kael raised his sword, his face set in grim determination. "Ready?"

Liora nodded, her chest tight with anticipation. "Do it."

With a shout, Kael brought his sword down on the stone, the blade cutting through the glowing runes with a sharp crack.

The moment the sword made contact, the air around them exploded with dark energy. The ground shook, the trees swaying violently as the magic was ripped from the stone, the connection between the creature and the forest severed.

The dark figure let out a deafening roar, its body trembling as the power drained from it. The shadows that had surrounded it began to dissipate, its form flickering like a dying flame.

Liora's heart raced as she watched the creature falter, its once overwhelming presence reduced to a flickering shadow.

"We did it," Kael muttered, his voice filled with disbelief.

But even as the creature weakened, Liora knew that the battle wasn't over. The dark figures still surrounded them, their eyes glowing with a malevolent light, and the magic in the air was still thick, still dangerous.

"We need to get out of here," Liora said, her voice tense. "Now."

Kael nodded, his eyes scanning the battlefield. "Fall back!"

The strike team moved quickly, their movements coordinated as they retreated from the clearing, cutting through the remaining dark figures as they made their way back toward the edge of the forest.

But even as they fled, Liora couldn't shake the feeling that this was just the beginning.

The shadows had found them.

And they weren't going to stop.

The sun was beginning to rise as the strike team emerged from the forest, their bodies weary from the battle, their faces grim. Liora's chest ached with exhaustion, her magic drained from the effort of fighting off the dark forces. Kael was at her side, his sword still in hand, his expression dark and filled with worry.

They had survived the battle. They had weakened the creature.

But the threat wasn't over.

As they reached the safety of Solstraea's walls, Kael turned to the soldiers, his voice steady but filled with tension. "We'll regroup at the palace. Prepare for whatever comes next."

Liora's heart tightened as she looked at him. She could see the weight of the battle pressing down on him, the fear that they hadn't done enough—that the darkness was still out there, waiting to strike again.

"You did everything you could," Liora said quietly, her hand resting on his arm. "We all did."

Kael's gaze softened, but there was a flicker of doubt in his eyes. "I just don't know if it'll be enough."

Liora's chest tightened with the weight of his words. She didn't have the answers, but she knew one thing for certain.

They weren't done fighting.

Not yet.

CHAPTER 13
THE DARKEST HOUR

The mood in the war room was heavy. Kael stood at the head of the table, his hands resting on the map of Solstraea that had been their constant reference since the dark forces had first appeared. Around him, the strike team sat in silence, their faces pale and drawn from the intensity of the battle in the Blackwood Forest.

Liora sat beside Kael, her heart still racing from the fight. Her body ached from the strain of using her magic, and her mind was clouded with fear. The victory they had claimed felt hollow. Yes, they had weakened the dark creature, but it wasn't enough. The shadow forces were still out there, and they were growing stronger.

"We managed to disrupt their magic," Callia said, breaking the silence. Her sharp eyes moved around the table, studying each face. "But this was only a temporary setback for them. They're going to come back. Stronger."

Kael's face darkened, his jaw tight with frustration. "We need to be ready. We need to figure out what they're after."

Liora's mind turned over the events of the battle, the creature's cryptic words still echoing in her head: *This kingdom will fall. And you will fall with it.*

"What do you think they meant when they said 'what was promised to them'?" Liora asked, her voice quiet but filled with urgency. "They keep referring to something that was owed to them."

Kael's brow furrowed, his eyes clouded with thought. "It's possible this goes back further than we realize. Something from the time before my father's reign."

Callia nodded thoughtfully. "I've been doing some research into the ancient records. There are mentions of a pact made long ago between the first rulers of Solstraea and a dark force—a pact that was never fulfilled."

Liora's pulse quickened. "A pact? What kind of pact?"

Callia sighed, her expression grim. "It's unclear. The records are fragmented, but there are references to a promise of power, of eternal life, that was never honored. If these dark forces are the remnants of that pact, they could be seeking revenge."

Kael's face tightened, his hand clenching into a fist on the table. "So, we're dealing with something from before our time—something tied to the kingdom's history."

Liora's chest tightened as the weight of that realization settled over her. This wasn't just about a battle for Solstraea's present. It was about a broken promise from the kingdom's past, and now, the shadows were coming to collect their due.

"We can't afford to wait any longer," Kael said, his voice firm. "If they're gathering strength, they'll be back sooner than we expect."

Callia nodded. "We need to find out exactly what they're after. If we can get to the heart of this pact, we might be able to stop them before they strike again."

Liora's heart raced as she listened to their plan form, but even as they spoke, a deep sense of dread gnawed at her insides. The dark forces had already proven they were relentless. This next battle would be different—more dangerous than anything they had faced before.

And she wasn't sure if they were ready for it.

After the war council adjourned, Kael retreated to the balcony overlooking the city. The sun was low in the sky, casting a golden light over the rooftops, but the beauty of the scene did little to ease the tension in his chest.

Liora joined him a few minutes later, her heart heavy with the weight of the decisions they had to make. She could feel the strain in him, the pressure of leadership bearing down on him like a storm cloud. He stood with his hands resting on the stone railing, his face turned toward the horizon, but his thoughts were distant.

"Kael?" Liora's voice was soft, hesitant.

Kael didn't turn to face her. "I've been thinking about what Callia said. About the pact."

Liora stepped closer, her chest tightening. "Do you think it's true? That this whole thing goes back to a promise made by your ancestors?"

Kael sighed, running a hand through his hair. "I don't know. But if it is... then I've inherited more than just a kingdom. I've inherited a broken promise, a curse that was never lifted."

Liora's heart ached as she listened to the pain in his voice. She reached out, her fingers brushing his arm gently. "This isn't your fault, Kael. You didn't ask for any of this."

Kael finally turned, meeting her gaze. The weariness in his eyes was unmistakable. "If it's going to break, it breaks with me."

Liora's heart ached, watching him shoulder a burden that seemed too heavy for one person. She stepped closer, her hand brushing against his arm. "It doesn't have to. We're stronger together."

Kael didn't respond at first, but his eyes softened, something unspoken passing between them. "I want to believe that."

Kael's gaze softened, his fingers tightening around hers. "I don't know if I can be the king Solstraea needs. I've spent so much of my life trapped in the Dreamplane, fighting against my father's curse. And now... this."

Liora's heart swelled with emotion as she looked up at him. "You've already proven you're a better king than your father ever was. You care about this kingdom, about your people. That's what makes you strong."

Kael's breath hitched, his eyes filled with gratitude and something deeper—something raw and vulnerable. "And what if I fail them? What if I fail you?"

Liora's chest tightened, her heart aching at the depth of his fears. She reached up, her hand resting against his cheek. "You won't. You're not alone in this, Kael. I'm with you. Always."

Kael's breath trembled as he leaned into her touch, his eyes searching hers. "I don't deserve you."

Liora's heart ached, and she shook her head. "Yes, you do."

For a long moment, they stood in silence, the weight of their connection grounding them in the midst of the storm brewing on the horizon. And in that moment, Liora realized that no matter what happened, no matter how dark the path ahead became, she would stand by Kael's side.

Together, they could face anything.

———

The next morning, the atmosphere in the palace was tense. The scouts had returned with grim news—large groups of dark figures were gathering at the edges of the Blackwood Forest, massing for what seemed like a coordinated attack. They were no longer content to hide in the shadows.

"They're planning to march on Solstraea," Callia said, her voice filled with urgency as she reported to Kael and Liora in the war room. "They're moving faster than we anticipated."

Kael's jaw tightened, his face set in a grim expression. "How long do we have?"

Callia hesitated, her eyes flicking to the map on the table. "A few days. Maybe less."

Liora's heart raced as she listened, her mind spinning with the reality of what they were facing. The dark forces weren't just going to attack—they were going to overrun Solstraea if they weren't stopped.

Kael's face darkened as he looked at the map. "We can't

wait for them to reach the city. We need to meet them head-on, outside the walls."

Liora's chest tightened at the thought of Kael leading an army into battle. She knew he was strong, that he had the heart of a warrior, but the dark magic they were facing was unlike anything they had ever seen. The memory of the creature in Blackwood still haunted her—the overwhelming power it had wielded, the suffocating presence of its magic.

"We'll need to gather every available soldier," Kael said, his voice filled with quiet determination. "This will be the fight for Solstraea's future."

Callia nodded. "I'll begin the preparations."

As she left the room, Liora turned to Kael, her heart pounding in her chest. "You're going to lead the charge, aren't you?"

Kael's gaze flicked to hers, his expression softening. "I have to. I can't ask my people to fight if I'm not willing to stand with them."

Liora's chest tightened with a mix of fear and pride. She knew Kael was right—he was a king who would lead by example, who would fight for his people with everything he had. But the thought of him facing the dark forces alone filled her with a sense of dread she couldn't shake.

"I'm coming with you," Liora said, her voice steady.

Kael's eyes widened slightly, and he shook his head. "No, Liora. It's too dangerous."

Liora stepped closer, her heart pounding with determination. "I've fought beside you before, and I'm not stopping now. You're not facing this alone."

Kael's gaze softened, but there was a flicker of fear in his eyes. "I can't lose you."

Liora's breath hitched, her chest tightening with emotion. "You won't."

For a long moment, they stood in silence, the weight of their unspoken fears hanging in the air between them. And then, with a quiet, tentative movement, Kael reached out, his hand slipping into hers.

"Then we face this together," he whispered, his voice trembling with emotion.

Liora nodded, her heart swelling with love and determination. "Together."

The preparations for battle moved quickly. The soldiers of Solstraea were called to arms, the city's defenses fortified, and Kael began rallying the troops for what would be the fight of their lives.

Liora spent most of her time helping where she could, her magic humming beneath her skin as she prepared herself for the battle ahead. She had fought before, but this was different. This wasn't just about survival. This was about defending everything she had come to care about—the kingdom, its people, and Kael.

The tension in the palace was palpable. Soldiers moved through the halls with grim expressions, their weapons gleaming in the dim light. Courtiers whispered in hushed voices, their faces pale with fear. The weight of the coming battle pressed down on everyone, and the sense of dread hung in the air like a thick fog.

As the day of the battle approached, Kael called a final meeting with his closest advisors and commanders. The war room was filled with the quiet murmur of voices, the tension so thick it was almost suffocating.

"We'll meet them just outside the city walls," Kael said, his voice steady but filled with the gravity of the situation. "We need to keep them from reaching Solstraea. If they breach the walls, we'll lose the city."

Callia nodded, her face set in a grim expression. "Our magic users will focus on disrupting their forces. We've seen how much their dark magic relies on coordination. If we can break their lines, we'll have a chance."

Kael's eyes flicked to Liora, and she could see the unspoken question in his gaze: *Are you ready?*

Liora's heart raced, but she nodded firmly. "I'm ready."

The rest of the meeting was spent finalizing the details of the strategy. Liora listened intently, her mind racing with the reality of what they were about to face. The battle ahead would be the most dangerous thing she had ever experienced, but she wasn't afraid. Not really.

Because she knew she wasn't alone.

The night before the battle was eerily quiet. The city of Solstraea had fallen into a tense silence, the streets empty, the air heavy with anticipation. The soldiers were preparing for the fight ahead, their movements quiet and efficient as they readied their weapons and armor.

Liora stood on the balcony of the palace, her eyes scanning the horizon. The Blackwood Forest loomed in the distance, dark and foreboding, like a shadow waiting to engulf the kingdom. Her heart pounded in her chest, her mind racing with thoughts of the battle ahead.

She heard footsteps behind her, and when she turned, Kael was standing in the doorway, his expression thoughtful.

"Can't sleep either?" Liora asked with a faint smile.

Kael shook his head, stepping onto the balcony beside her. "Too much to think about."

Liora's chest tightened as she looked up at him. "You're going to make it through this, Kael. We both are."

Kael's gaze softened, but there was a flicker of doubt in his eyes. "What if I can't protect everyone? What if—"

Liora reached out, her hand resting against his chest. "You're not alone in this. You have your people. You have me. We'll get through it."

Kael's breath trembled as he looked down at her, his eyes filled with a mixture of fear and love. "I don't know what I'd do without you."

Liora smiled softly, her heart swelling with emotion. "You'll never have to find out."

For a long moment, they stood in silence, the weight of their connection grounding them in the midst of the storm they were about to face. And in that moment, Liora knew that no matter what happened, no matter how dark the path ahead became, she and Kael would face it together.

And they would survive.

CHAPTER 14

BATTLE FOR SOLSTRAEA

The sun had not yet risen when the soldiers of Solstraea gathered outside the city gates. The air was thick with tension, the morning mist swirling around their feet as they prepared for the battle ahead. Liora stood among them, her heart pounding in her chest as she adjusted the strap of her armor, the weight of her dagger pressing against her hip. The thorns beneath her skin hummed with energy, reacting to the dark magic that loomed on the horizon.

Kael was beside her, dressed in his royal armor, his sword gleaming in the dim light. His face was set in a grim expression, but Liora could see the determination in his eyes. He was ready. They all were.

As the soldiers finished their preparations, Kael mounted his horse, his voice carrying over the quiet field. "Today, we fight for Solstraea," he said, his voice strong and steady. "We fight to protect our people, our home. The darkness is coming, but we will not let it take us."

The soldiers raised their weapons in silent agreement, their faces grim but resolute. Liora felt a surge of pride as she watched them—these men and women who had given everything to protect their kingdom.

"We'll move quickly," Kael said, turning to Liora and Callia, who stood nearby. "The dark forces are still gathering near the Blackwood. If we strike first, we might be able to disrupt their magic before they reach the city."

Callia nodded, her eyes sharp. "Their strength lies in their coordinated efforts. If we focus our magic on weakening their lines, they'll fall apart."

Liora's pulse quickened, her mind racing with the gravity of what was about to happen. This was it. The battle that would decide the future of Solstraea.

"We'll be right behind you," Kael said quietly, his gaze flicking to Liora. "But stay close. I don't want you taking any unnecessary risks."

Liora smirked, her heart pounding with a mixture of fear and determination. "I could say the same to you."

Kael's eyes softened, and for a moment, the weight of everything seemed to fall away. "We'll get through this," he whispered, his voice filled with quiet certainty. "Together."

Liora nodded, her chest tight with emotion. "Together."

With that, the command was given, and the army of Solstraea began to move. The soldiers marched in formation, their steps silent but heavy with purpose, the sound of their armor clinking faintly in the early morning air. The tension was palpable, every face set with grim resolve as they approached the battlefield.

The Blackwood Forest loomed ahead, dark and ominous against the pale light of dawn. Liora could feel the dark magic pulsing from the trees, the shadows shifting and moving like living creatures as they prepared to face the oncoming army.

The battle for Solstraea had begun.

The moment they reached the edge of the forest, the air seemed to explode with dark energy.

Figures emerged from the shadows, cloaked in black, their eyes glowing with the same eerie light Liora had seen before. The dark forces moved quickly, their bodies shifting like shadows as they closed in on Solstraea's army.

"Here they come!" Kael shouted, raising his sword. "Hold the line!"

The soldiers reacted instantly, their weapons raised as they formed a defensive wall, their faces set in grim determination. The clash of metal rang out as the two forces met, the sound of swords and shields echoing through the forest.

Liora's magic flared to life as she threw herself into the fight, her dagger slicing through the air with deadly precision. The thorns beneath her skin surged with energy, snapping at the dark figures as they lunged toward her.

The battle was chaos. The dark forces moved with terrifying speed, their bodies shifting and twisting as they dodged attacks with unnatural grace. But the soldiers of Solstraea held their ground, their weapons flashing as they fought back against the overwhelming force of the shadows.

Liora's heart raced as she fought, her body moving on

instinct. She had been in battles before, but nothing like this. The air was thick with magic, the dark energy pressing down on her like a weight, suffocating her. She could feel the darkness closing in, but she pushed it back, her magic pulsing with every strike.

"Liora, behind you!" Kael's voice cut through the chaos, and Liora spun just in time to block an attack from one of the shadow figures.

The creature's blade clashed against her dagger, the force of it sending a shockwave through her body. But Liora held firm, her magic surging as she pushed back, the thorns snapping around the creature and pulling it to the ground.

Kael was at her side in an instant, his sword slicing through the air as he fought off another attacker. "Stay with me!" he shouted over the noise of the battle.

"I'm not going anywhere!" Liora shouted back, her breath ragged.

They fought side by side, their movements fluid and coordinated, but the dark forces seemed endless. For every figure they cut down, two more appeared from the shadows, their eyes glowing with malevolent intent.

"We need to break their lines!" Callia shouted from behind them, her hands glowing with magical energy as she cast a spell that sent a blast of light toward the dark figures. "They're overwhelming us!"

Kael's face was set in a grim expression as he blocked another attack. "Liora, we need your magic. We have to weaken them."

Liora's pulse quickened, her heart racing with the

weight of his words. She knew what he was asking. She had to use her full power—everything she had—to disrupt the dark magic that fueled the enemy. But it was risky. She didn't know if she had the strength to control it.

But she didn't have a choice.

Taking a deep breath, Liora focused her energy, the thorns beneath her skin snapping to attention as her magic flared to life. She could feel the dark magic pressing against her, but she pushed back, her power surging through her like a river.

With a shout, Liora unleashed her magic, the thorns spreading out around her like a web of vines. They lashed out at the dark figures, wrapping around them, cutting through the shadows with deadly precision. The air crackled with energy as the thorns pierced the darkness, disrupting the enemy's coordination, weakening their lines.

The effect was immediate.

The dark forces faltered, their movements slowing as the magic that held them together began to unravel. The soldiers of Solstraea pushed forward, taking advantage of the opening Liora had created, their swords flashing as they cut through the enemy ranks.

"We're breaking them!" Kael shouted, his eyes wide with hope.

Liora's heart leapt in her chest, her magic still pulsing with energy. They were winning. They were pushing back the darkness.

But then, from the heart of the forest, a figure emerged.

The battlefield fell into an eerie silence as the figure stepped out from the shadows. It was cloaked in black, its face hidden beneath a dark hood, but Liora could feel the overwhelming power radiating from it.

Kael's face darkened, his sword raised as he stepped in front of Liora. "That's their leader."

Liora's heart raced as she looked at the figure, her magic humming with tension. The dark forces had faltered when her magic had disrupted them, but this figure—it was different. It wasn't just another shadow creature. It was the source of the dark magic that had been haunting them, the force behind the attack on Solstraea.

The figure's voice was low and menacing, like the whisper of dead leaves in the wind. "You cannot stop what is already in motion, King of Solstraea."

Kael's jaw clenched, his sword gleaming in the dim light. "I won't let you destroy my kingdom."

The figure tilted its head slightly, its glowing eyes fixed on Kael. "Your kingdom was doomed the moment the pact was broken."

Liora's breath caught in her throat, her heart pounding. *The pact.* The broken promise that had led to all of this. But how could they stop it now?

"You don't have to do this," Liora shouted, stepping forward. "We can find another way. You don't have to destroy everything."

The figure's gaze flicked to her, and for a moment, the air seemed to freeze. "There is no other way," it said quietly. "This kingdom's fate was sealed long ago. The shadows will take what is owed."

Liora's pulse quickened, her magic flaring as she stepped in front of Kael. "I won't let that happen."

The figure's eyes glowed brighter, and it raised its hand, dark energy swirling around its fingers. "Then you will fall with it."

Before anyone could react, the figure unleashed a blast of dark magic, the force of it slamming into Liora like a wave. She stumbled back, her body trembling with the effort of holding it off, her magic straining under the weight of the attack.

"Liora!" Kael shouted, rushing to her side.

But Liora held up a hand, her chest tight with determination. "I'm fine," she said through gritted teeth. "I can do this."

With a deep breath, Liora pushed back, her magic flaring to life as the thorns wrapped around her like a shield. She could feel the dark magic pressing against her, but she didn't let it break her. She was stronger than the darkness. She had to be.

The figure tilted its head again, watching her with something like curiosity. "Impressive. But it will not be enough."

Kael's face was set in a grim expression as he raised his sword. "We'll see about that."

The battle raged around them, but all Liora could see was the dark figure standing before her, its magic pulsing through the air like a storm. Her body ached from the strain of holding off its attacks, but she couldn't stop. Not now.

Kael was at her side, his sword flashing as he deflected another blast of dark energy. "We need to find its weakness," he muttered, his voice tight with concentration.

Liora nodded, her mind racing. There had to be something—some way to disrupt the figure's power, to break the connection between it and the dark magic that fueled it. But what?

And then, she saw it.

The figure's hand—the one it had raised to cast its spells—was marked with the same glowing runes they had seen on the stone in Blackwood. The source of its power.

"The runes!" Liora shouted, her voice filled with urgency. "It's using them to channel the magic!"

Kael's eyes widened as he followed her gaze. "Then we destroy them."

Liora's heart raced as she focused her magic, the thorns snapping to attention. If she could disrupt the runes, she could weaken the figure. But it wouldn't be easy.

Taking a deep breath, Liora unleashed her magic, the thorns lashing out at the figure's hand, wrapping around its wrist. The figure hissed, its body trembling as the thorns tightened, the dark magic crackling around it.

But the figure wasn't done.

With a low growl, it raised its other hand, a blast of dark energy shooting toward Liora with terrifying speed.

Kael moved before she could react, his sword flashing as he blocked the attack, the force of it sending him stumbling back. "Liora, now!"

Liora's heart pounded as she tightened her grip on the

thorns, her running through her veins. She could feel the runes weakening, the dark magic faltering under the strain of her power.

And then, with a final burst of energy, the runes shattered.

The figure let out a deafening roar as the dark magic exploded around it, the shadows twisting and writhing like living creatures as they were ripped apart.

Liora stumbled back, her body trembling with exhaustion, but she didn't stop. She couldn't stop. Not yet.

With a shout, Kael raised his sword and struck the final blow, his blade slicing through the air as it cut through the figure's chest.

The dark figure let out one final, piercing scream before it crumbled to the ground, its body dissolving into shadows that faded into the air.

The battlefield fell silent.

The dark forces had been broken. The moment their leader fell, the remaining shadow creatures had dissolved into the wind, their bodies crumbling like dust. The soldiers of Solstraea stood in stunned silence, their weapons still raised, their bodies trembling from the intensity of the battle.

Liora's legs gave out, and she sank to her knees, her chest heaving as she tried to catch her breath. The thorns beneath her skin were still humming with energy, but the exhaustion was overwhelming. She had pushed herself to the limit—used every ounce of her magic to stop the dark figure.

Kael was at her side in an instant, his arms wrapping around her as he helped her to her feet. "Liora," he whispered, his voice filled with worry. "Are you alright?"

Liora nodded weakly, her body trembling. "I'm fine," she said, though her voice was barely above a whisper. "Just... tired."

Kael's face was filled with relief, but his eyes were still clouded with worry. "You did it. You broke their magic."

Liora smiled faintly, her heart swelling with emotion. "We did it. Together."

For a long moment, they stood in silence, the weight of the battle settling over them. The dark forces were gone, the shadows defeated. Solstraea had been saved.

But the cost had been great.

As they looked out over the battlefield, the bodies of fallen soldiers littered the ground, a grim reminder of the price they had paid for victory. The city had survived, but not without sacrifice.

Kael's face darkened as he looked at the destruction, his chest tight with emotion. "So many lives lost," he muttered, his voice filled with pain.

Liora's heart ached as she followed his gaze, the weight of the loss pressing down on her. "But they didn't die in vain. They died protecting their home."

Kael nodded, his eyes filled with quiet determination. "We'll honor them."

Liora's chest tightened with emotion, and she reached out, her hand slipping into his. "We will."

As the sun began to rise over the battlefield, casting the

world in a soft, golden light, Liora knew that they had won. They had defeated the darkness, broken the pact that had haunted Solstraea for centuries.

But the scars of the battle would linger.

And they would never forget the price they had paid for their victory.

CHAPTER 15
A KINGDOM REBORN

The first light of dawn broke over the city of Solstraea, casting the world in a soft, golden glow. The air was crisp, still carrying the faint scent of smoke from the battle, but the sound of rebuilding had already begun. Soldiers moved through the streets, helping to clear debris and tend to the wounded. The people of Solstraea were shaken but alive, their spirits unbroken.

Liora stood on the balcony of the palace, looking out over the city below. Her body ached from the battle, her magic drained, but there was a quiet peace in the air that made her heart swell. They had survived. Solstraea had survived.

But the cost had been high.

Kael joined her a moment later, his footsteps quiet as he stepped up beside her. His face was somber, his eyes scanning the horizon, but there was a calmness in him that hadn't been there before. He had grown into his role as king—not just in title, but in spirit.

"The city will heal," Kael said quietly, his voice steady.

Liora nodded, her chest tight with emotion. "It will. But it won't be easy."

Kael's gaze softened, and he turned to face her. "We'll rebuild. Together."

Liora smiled faintly, her heart swelling with love for him. She had fought beside him through everything— through the curse, the dark forces, the battle for the kingdom—and now, they were standing on the other side of it. Stronger. Together.

For a long moment, they stood in silence, the weight of the battle still hanging in the air around them. But there was also hope—a sense of renewal that filled the morning light, a promise of something better to come.

"You've been quiet," Kael said softly, his eyes searching hers. "What's on your mind?"

Liora sighed, her chest tightening with the weight of her thoughts. "I was just thinking about everything that's happened. About all the people we lost."

Kael's face darkened, his jaw tightening. "I know. It's hard to think about."

Liora's heart ached as she looked at him. She could see the pain in his eyes—the weight of every life lost, every sacrifice made. He carried it with him, even now, in the quiet moments after the battle.

"But they didn't die for nothing," Liora said, her voice filled with quiet conviction. "They died protecting their home. And because of them, Solstraea has a future."

Kael's gaze softened, and he nodded slowly. "You're right. They won't be forgotten."

Liora smiled faintly, her heart swelling with emotion. "We will."

As they stood together on the balcony, the sun rising higher in the sky, Liora knew that this was the beginning of something new. The darkness had passed, the shadows had been defeated, and now, they had the chance to rebuild—to create a future that was better, stronger, and filled with hope.

———

The days that followed were filled with the work of rebuilding. The palace, the city, and the kingdom itself had all been scarred by the battle, but there was a sense of unity that ran through Solstraea like a lifeline. The people came together, working side by side to repair what had been broken, their determination as strong as ever.

Liora spent her days helping wherever she could—tending to the wounded, organizing supplies, and offering her magic where it was needed. But more than that, she felt a deep connection to the people of Solstraea. They were no longer strangers to her. This kingdom had become her home, and its people, her family.

Kael was always at the center of the effort. He moved through the city with a quiet grace, offering words of encouragement, lending his strength to the rebuilding, and guiding the people through the aftermath of the battle. He had become the king Solstraea needed—a leader who didn't just rule from the palace, but rather one who stood with his people, through every hardship, every victory.

One afternoon, as Liora was helping to distribute food to the workers in the city square, she heard Kael's voice behind her.

"You've been busy."

Liora turned, a faint smile tugging at her lips as she saw him standing there, his expression soft. "So have you," she said with a smirk. "Isn't this supposed to be your day off?"

Kael chuckled, his eyes twinkling with amusement. "Kings don't get days off. Or so I've been told."

Liora laughed, her heart lightened by the sound of his voice. For the first time in what felt like forever, there was a sense of ease between them—a lightness that hadn't been there during the battle, or even before it. The weight of the curse, the dark magic, the fear of what was to come —it was all behind them now. And in its place, there was hope.

Kael stepped closer, his hand slipping into hers. "I'm proud of you, you know," he said quietly, his voice filled with sincerity.

Liora's heart swelled with emotion. "Proud of me? I think you're the one who deserves the praise."

Kael's eyes softened, and he shook his head. "We both fought for this kingdom. I couldn't have done any of it without you."

Liora's breath hitched, her chest tightening with the depth of his words. She had fought beside him, but she hadn't done it for the kingdom alone. She had done it for him. For them.

And now, standing here in the heart of Solstraea, with Kael's hand in hers, she knew that whatever came next— whatever challenges they faced—they would face it together.

"Kael," she whispered, her voice trembling with emotion. "I—"

But before she could finish, Kael leaned in, his lips brushing hers in a soft, tender kiss.

The world seemed to fall away in that moment. The city, the people, the noise—all of it faded into the background as Liora lost herself in the warmth of Kael's touch, the gentle press of his lips against hers. It wasn't the first time they had kissed, but this time, it felt different. It felt like a promise—a quiet, unspoken vow that they would always stand together, no matter what.

When they finally pulled apart, Kael's eyes were filled with something raw, something real. "I love you, Liora," he whispered, his voice trembling with sincerity.

Liora's heart swelled, her chest tight with emotion. "I love you, too," she whispered back, her voice barely audible.

For a long moment, they stood in silence, their hands intertwined, the world around them quiet and still. And in that moment, Liora knew that they had found something worth fighting for. Something stronger than magic, stronger than the darkness that had once threatened to tear them apart.

They had found each other.

The people of Solstraea, guided by Kael's leadership, began to repair the damage done by the battle, slowly restoring the city to its former glory. The scars of the conflict would remain, but they were a testament to the strength of the kingdom—a reminder of the sacrifices made to protect their home.

Liora found herself settling into her new life in the palace, though it was nothing like the life she had once imagined for herself. She had grown up on the streets, a thief and an outcast, never dreaming that she would one day stand at the side of a king. But here she was, and for the first time in a long time, she felt at peace.

One afternoon, as she wandered through the palace gardens, she found Kael sitting on a stone bench, his face turned up to the sun. He looked relaxed, his body at ease in a way that she hadn't seen in months.

"You look content," Liora said with a smirk as she approached.

Kael opened one eye, a lazy smile spreading across his lips. "That's because I am."

Liora laughed, her heart light. She sat beside him, her hand resting gently on his arm. "We've come a long way, haven't we?"

Kael nodded, his gaze thoughtful. "We have. But I wouldn't change any of it."

Liora's chest tightened with emotion as she looked at him. "Neither would I."

For a long moment, they sat in comfortable silence, the warmth of the sun and the sound of the birds in the garden wrapping around them like a soft embrace. The world had been through so much darkness, but here, in this quiet moment, there was only light.

Kael turned to her, his eyes filled with quiet affection. "I want to build something with you, Liora. A life. A future."

Liora's heart skipped a beat, her breath catching in her throat. "You already have."

Kael smiled softly, his hand slipping into hers. "I meant something more. Something lasting."

Liora's chest swelled with emotion, her eyes locking with his. "I want that too."

And in that moment, Liora knew that this was the beginning of something beautiful. They had faced the darkness together, fought through the shadows, and now, they had the chance to create something new. A kingdom reborn, built on hope, love, and the promise of a future they would face side by side.

As the months passed, the kingdom of Solstraea continued to heal. The scars of the battle slowly faded, and the city began to thrive once more. Under Kael's leadership, the people found strength in their unity, their hearts filled with the hope of a brighter future.

Liora became an integral part of the rebuilding effort, using her magic to help where she could and offering her support to the people of Solstraea. She had once been an outsider, but now, she was part of something bigger—something that gave her a sense of purpose and belonging.

Kael led his people with the quiet strength and grace that had always been a part of him, but now, there was a confidence in him that hadn't been there before. He had proven himself as king, not just in battle, but in the way he cared for his people, the way he fought for their future.

Together, Kael and Liora stood at the heart of Solstraea,

a symbol of hope and resilience in a kingdom that had been through so much.

One evening, as the sun began to set over the city, Liora stood on the balcony of the palace, looking out over the streets below. The lights of the city twinkled in the fading light, and for the first time in a long time, there was a sense of peace in the air.

Kael joined her, his arm slipping around her waist as he pulled her close. "It's beautiful, isn't it?" he asked softly, his voice filled with quiet wonder.

Liora nodded, her heart swelling with love for him. "It is."

For a long moment, they stood in silence, the warmth of the setting sun wrapping around them like a blanket. And in that moment, Liora knew that they had found something lasting—something that would carry them through whatever challenges lay ahead.

They had built a kingdom united.

And together, they would face whatever came next.

The night was quiet as Liora and Kael stood in the palace garden, the soft glow of the moon casting a silver light over the flowers and trees. The air was cool, the scent of blooming roses filling the air, but the warmth of Kael's hand in hers made Liora feel at peace.

"I never thought I'd end up here," Liora said softly, her voice filled with quiet wonder. "In a place like this."

Kael smiled, his eyes filled with affection. "Neither did I."

Liora chuckled, her heart light. "But I wouldn't change any of it."

Kael's gaze softened, and he leaned in, his lips brushing hers in a soft, lingering kiss. "Neither would I."

As they stood together under the moonlit sky, Liora knew that no matter what challenges lay ahead, no matter what darkness might rise in the future, they would face it together. Their bond was unbreakable, their love stronger than any curse, any battle.

And they would always be together.

Always.

Did you enjoy Liora and Kael's story?
Please rate or review it on Goodreads, Bookbub or your favourite retailer.

Read *A Curse of Glass and Shadows* , the next book in the *Legends Reborn* series.

For updates, sales, and promotions, join my newsletter at mhlebeaultauthor.substack.com

ABOUT THE AUTHOR

Positive, uplifting books and stories.

Marie-Hélène Lebeault is the author of *The Evers Series,
Clarity Castle, What Happens Next? Readers Decide Which
Story Becomes a Book, the Blood Magick Trilogy, Holiday
Shifters, Ghost Stories, Defenders of the Realm, Utopia,
Chronicles of the Starborne Cadets*, as well as a series of
picture books called Fairy Grandmother. She lives in
Canada with her grown children.

www.mhlebeault.com

Follow on Social Media, she'd love to hear from you!

facebook.com/mhlebeaultauthor
x.com/mhlebeault
instagram.com/mhlebeault
amazon.com/author/mhlebeault
bookbub.com/authors/marie-helene-lebeault
goodreads.com/mhlebeault
linkedin.com/in/mhlebeault
tiktok.com/@mhlebeaultauthor

Also by the Author

Legends Reborn (Fairytale Retellings)

A Curse of Snow and Ash

A Curse of Thorns and Slumber

A Curse of Glass and Shadows

A Curse of Silver and Scars

A Curse of Storm and Stone

A Curse of Sand and Smoke

The Chronicles of the Starborne Cadets

Confluence of Destinies

Stars Beyond Realms

Shadows of Orion

Echoes of the Void

The Nebula's Heart

The Starborne Paradox

Defenders of the Realm

A Journey to Power

The Quest for the Emerald Rattleback

A Summer of Discovery

The Quest for the Sacred Tree

A Summer of Opposites

The Quest for the Phantom Feather

A Summer of Courage

The Quest for the Kraken's Ink

A Summer of Destiny

The Quest for the Cursed Mirrors

A Summer of Unity

Defenders of the Realm - Special Edition Hardcover Set

The Battle of the Blossoming Flame (FREE!)

The Evers Series

The Ancestors' Key

The Academy

The Time Walker

The World Jumper

5th Anniversary Edition Omnibus

The Traveler's Handbook

The Lost Key

Blood Magick Trilogy

The Blood Mage

Blood Magick

Blood Legacy

Extended Edition Omnibus

Standalones

Clarity Castle

What Happens Next?

Ghost Stories

Holiday Shifters

Echoes of Tomorrow

Utopia

Picture Books

Fairy Grandmother: Millie Goes to Antarctica

Fairy Grandmother: Millie Goes to the North Pole

Fairy Grandmother: Millie Goes to China

Fairy Grandmother: Millie Goes to Africa

(Also available in French, Spanish, German, and Italian)